THE GOSSIPING GOURMET

A MURDER IN MARIN MYSTERY – BOOK 1

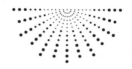

MARTIN BROWN

A BOOK BY

SIGNAL
PRESS

Library of Congress Cataloging-in-Publication Data is available upon request

Cover Design by Andrew Brown, ClickTwiceDesign.com

Book Formatting by Austin Brown, CheapEbookFormatting.com

Trade Paperback ISBN: 978-1-942052-44-9

V102619

CHAPTER ONE

On the first Monday of every month, Warren Bradley, community newspaper columnist extraordinaire, catered a lunchtime feast for Sausalito's men and women in blue. His generous offer was driven by selfish reasons. Bradley was always in search of scandal and did not object if the information he dredged up lacked context, provided it came with a healthy portion of innuendo, supposition, and plausible conjecture.

Headquartered in a two-story building that took up an entire block at the end of Caledonia Street, Sausalito's self-proclaimed "resident-serving commercial district," the police department had a state-of-the-art lockdown area, a meeting room with richly appointed mahogany walls, and a workout facility that was the envy of all other Marin County police departments. All at the disposal of a force of two dozen uniformed officers, five support staff, a chief, and a deputy chief. It was undoubtedly more police coverage than any town of seven thousand required—particularly given that the county sheriff's department maintained a Southern Marin station just two miles north of Sausalito's lavish police headquarters.

The fire station, on the opposite side of the street, was equally grand. Day visitors, which Sausalito attracted on summer weekends by the thousands, often mistook its massive windows and antique brickwork for the front of a luxury hotel. But firefighters, in spite of their opulent surroundings, were never treated to Warren's garden of culinary delights. When Bea, one of Warren's compatriots in the game of know-and-tell, asked why he worked so hard to accommodate the local police, but not Sausalito's firefighters, he explained, "Grease fires and cats stuck in trees are of little interest to me or my readers."

For Sausalito's finest, however, he prepared his best dishes, and they reciprocated with unexpected delicious morsels of salacious details that raised his standing in a social circle above his actual station in life, and made the hours of shopping, preparation, cooking, carrying, and serving all worthwhile.

The department's rank and file much appreciated his efforts, from Captain Hans Petersen down to the city's newest patrol officer, Chris Harding, who had escaped policing the mean streets of San Jose for the quieter, and safer, surroundings of Sausalito.

Warren's gourmet lunches were the highlight of the department's month for those who normally subsisted on diets of Arby's and Subway sandwiches. Officers who might have called in sick that day, with plans to go deep sea fishing or out to Peacock Gap to play eighteen holes of golf, chose other days to be stricken with an unexpected case of "blue flu." Chief Petersen was particularly impressed when officers with the day off showed up around eleven forty-five, to get something they had "forgotten" out of their lockers.

As a connoisseur of indiscreet conversation, Warren made sure that when the food was plated, he would be first to the table, anxious to catch any new gossip. Sometimes, it was nothing more than a small gem, like a 415 call—disturbing the peace—caused by one or both of the mayor's drunken teenage sons.

And, sometimes, it was a precious stone. Case in point: the assault and battery arrest of Grant Randolph, chair of the Sausalito Fine Arts Commission. In that instance, his timing could not have been better. Twelve hours after Randolph was booked into the county jail, Warren busied himself preparing his caramel chicken. Eighteen pounds of chicken legs and thighs marinated in a sauce of light brown sugar, peeled ginger, rice vinegar, soy sauce, and vegetable oil—a blend of fantastic tastes that nearly brought every hardworking law enforcement officer to tears.

The night of Randolph's arrest, Harding and his partner, Steve Hansen, were the first two officers on the scene. Between bites and praise of Warren's chicken, Harding said, "The EMT boys had to take Randolph's wife up to the hospital."

"She was in pretty bad shape when we arrived," Hansen added.

All at once the tips of Warren's ears tingled as he stopped to contemplate the value of this news. Randolph seemed to take delight in correcting Warren at every one of their encounters. Perhaps the tables were finally about to turn.

Warren's upper lip, which balanced an unruly salt and pepper mustache, puckered forward with a laugh when he heard the surprising news. "No, I don't believe that! Really?

Grant Randolph? I didn't think he would hurt a fly, even if he seems to be built like someone who could."

"You'd know he could pack a wallop if you had seen Mrs. Randolph flat on her back, sprawled across their living room floor," Harding replied.

"Wow," Warren murmured, as he proffered another piece of sweet and spicy chicken to his new favorite police officer.

Warren's aging social set considered Randolph a bit too aggressive. Undoubtedly, he had the right pedigree in the arts, and his financial standing was beyond question, but accepting the chairmanship of the town's art commission when he had taken up residence only months earlier seemed presumptuous.

If it had not been for the fact that no one else was interested in investing the time and effort needed to do the job, with the likely exception of Warren himself, Randolph would not have been handed the position without objection.

Mrs. Alma Samuels, who had been married to the late San Francisco attorney Roger Samuels, also thought Randolph was a bit presumptuous. But she tolerated the man because, as she explained, "he has unquestioned credentials in the world of fine art." However, she shared with Warren and her close group of friends, known locally as the Ladies of Liberty—Ethel Landau, Marilyn Williams, Bea Snyder, and Robin Mitchell— that she too felt uncomfortable with the man she often referred to as "an east coast know-it-all" (an opinion that grew in Alma's mind from a seed planted there by Warren).

Armed with this shocking bit of news, Warren knew it would not be long before word of Randolph's arrest was whispered loudly into Alma's one good ear. The hearing in the aging widow's right ear had been gone almost as long as her husband.

Best of all, news of Grant's arrest would be the perfect item to lead Warren's column, "Heard About Town," which appeared in the town's only newspaper, *The Sausalito Standard*.

But, was it wise to be so hasty? Would it be a waste of a delicious piece of gossip that could be doled out more carefully? Warren wondered as the room buzzed with a half dozen different conversations.

Fortunately for Warren, the paper's publisher, Rob Timmons, was not on the best of terms with Chief Petersen, having written one too many stories about unsolved residential burglaries in Sausalito.

"The guy's a muckraker," Petersen complained to Warren on numerous occasions. "If his family hadn't lived in Sausalito for three generations, and his father hadn't been the town's fire chief for thirty years, no one would pay attention to what he wrote in that weekly rag of his."

Rob had long known that Chief Petersen preferred he write about anything but Sausalito's finest. Unfortunately, their bloated budget and the repeated bumbling of various cases made them an irresistible target. Among the citizens of Sausalito, complaints about their police department had long been a cause for debate. Nearly all of those who were home by nine and in bed by ten thought their police did an outstanding job. But those who lived a more active life, crossing the Golden Gate Bridge for the short drive into San Francisco for the symphony, the theater, or various social events, thought differently.

Traveling through Sausalito after eleven o'clock at night could be risky. Patrol officers, who were expected to issue a certain number of traffic citations during an eight-hour shift, would pull over vehicles for such offenses as a "rolling stop," as opposed to making a full stop at one of the city's endless gauntlet of stop signs.

The careful policing of traffic violations was particularly galling to someone who arrived home minutes after being stopped by a patrol officer, only to find their house had been burglarized.

Incidents like these led to a steady flurry of reader letters to *The Standard* complaining that, "Sausalito's well-paid police are busily working speed traps while thieves are cleaning out our homes of jewelry and other valuables."

Rob knew that his often-critical coverage of the Sausalito PD pleased many of the town's most successful individuals. People who in turn would make a point to patronize local merchants, and who were not shy in expressing their support for the "good work of Sausalito's community newspaper."

Rob's less-than-cordial relationship with Petersen's police force was counterbalanced by his close relationship with the county sheriff's department, where his former high school basketball teammate and longtime best friend, Eddie Austin, served as the department's lead investigator.

Eddie shared Rob's view that the Sausalito PD was "the gang that couldn't shoot straight." He and Rob also knew the situation was exacerbated by the two departments having jurisdictions that bordered one another.

It was always a tightrope walk for Warren—the what, where, when, how, and who of dishing the dirt. Many factors had to be taken into consideration. Keeping secrets from one, sharing them with another, while laying out a plan of attack. All the while remaining aware that telling too little meant not holding his audience's attention. But telling too much meant losing control of whatever bit of gossip was in his grasp that given week.

Warren tantalized his loyal followers with a blend of half-truths, disregarding Mark Twain's sage advice, "If you tell the truth, you don't have to remember anything." Understandably, Warren was always pressed to recall what he had said and with whom he had shared his noxious blend of truth and assumption.

Later that afternoon, hours after his caramel chicken was both praised and devoured, Warren sat in a small nook in his spare, one-bedroom cottage. His aging fingers were curled menacingly over a keyboard where many of the letters had all but faded from view. Fortunately for him he knew the position of every key by heart, and any letter hit in error appeared on a monochrome monitor that by logic should have gone dark several years earlier. Poised to strike at his prey, Warren ached to tap out the name Grant Randolph. But an uncertainty welled up inside of him, and he paused.

With little time before his deadline, he chose, as he had previously, to fill his column with a mix of his usual reflections: the amusing differences between cats and dogs; the need to keep our "small city's streets tidy in spite of the daily abuse they encounter as hordes of tourists trample through downtown, carelessly discarding unfinished ice cream cones, ketchup packets, hamburger and hot dog wrappers!"

Warren concluded with a lament about the woeful absence of manners in today's youth. "We were raised to respect our neighbors' right to quiet and privacy. Has kindness and consideration disappeared completely?" Warren asked in a fever pitch, certain his latest offering would please adoring readers.

Each Wednesday, when *The Sausalito Standard* containing his latest mix of rumor and admonishments landed in every mailbox in town, Warren anticipated several calls from admirers praising his latest efforts. But while praise was the expressed purpose of their call, most had only one question: "Warren, what do you hear in your travels through town?" And since most of these callers were age eighty or older, Warren was in the habit of speaking up.

His usual approach was to start with a question: For example, "Did you know that Penelope Jones is planning to remarry?"

His caller might respond, "Why, I didn't think her divorce had been finalized!"

"That was my first thought," Warren added with a short laugh.

From that point, the conversation would devolve into speculation.

Warren: "Bill Butler is going to need a hip replacement. I was wondering, do you think his wife pushed him down the stairs, or that he just fell down drunk on his own?"

Caller: "Oh, Warren, you're so right! That man's life would improve greatly if he gave up the bottle."

Warren's phone circle always included longtime members of the Sausalito Women's League. Simply known as "The League," it started back in the early years of the twentieth century and was organized as a clandestine effort to support the suffragette movement. Over the intervening years, the organization grew into the paramount social set for Sausalito's established gentry.

Alma Samuels' service as president emeritus was all the proof needed of the club's continued high standing.

In 1976, in recognition of the American Bicentennial, Samuels—who was the one person in Sausalito in whom social and political power reached its pinnacle—formed her own tight-knit circle, which she called the Ladies of Liberty, of whom Marilyn Williams, age 72, was today its youngest member.

Within this group, Bradley's columns were received with a blend of giggles and false admonishments. "Oh, Warren, you're just awful!" they'd tease after he put into print a particularly nasty piece of gossip.

He'd chuckle in a conspiratorial tone and declare, "I suppose I just can't help myself!"

Early each week, before his column was due, Warren's phone would ring. Invariably, Alma Samuels was the caller. This served as Warren's opportunity to invite himself up to her expansive and sadly empty mansion atop one of Sausalito's highest points. From that lofty height, the views of Richardson Bay were a breathtaking collage of blue water and white sails, against the backdrop of the Tiburon Peninsula's rolling green hills and opulent estates.

"Alma," Warren said in a volume a bit higher and certainly more ominous than usual, "you will not believe the trouble Grant Randolph has gotten himself into. It's too delicious to tell you over the phone. I have to see your reaction with my own eyes."

"Well, what are you waiting for? Get yourself up here," Alma croaked, and then announced, with a flirtatious giggle, "Prying minds need to know!"

CHAPTER TWO

The Samuels mansion sat on a leveled lot up near the top of Monte Mar Drive. The street was less traveled than many other roads in Sausalito, all of which eventually led down to the bay and the tourist-impacted part of the small town of seventy-two hundred souls.

Its absence of traffic was one of the pluses that attracted Roger and Alma Samuels to purchase the home in 1967, well before Sausalito emerged from what many thought of as the dark days of the counterculture, highlighted by San Francisco's infamous Summer of Love.

During that era, the Samuels rarely visited the small downtown where, on weekends, hippies often stripped down to their underwear, or less, and frolicked in the fountain that graced the small, green, palm tree-lined city center park, Vina Del Mar. (Twenty-five years later, one of those nude bathers served a term as the city's mayor—a topic rarely discussed in polite society.)

The Samuels homestead had been in desperate need of

repair. But both Alma and Roger—a securities attorney who had a cold, distant heart and a keen mind—could see its enormous potential. The house sat on a beautiful piece of land, with broad vistas that stretched from Mount Tamalpais to the north, Berkeley to the east, and San Francisco to the south. The iconic Golden Gate Bridge was not visible because of the Marin Headlands to its southwest, but the views it did have were picture-postcard worthy. And so, the up-and-coming attorney and his adoring wife took a chance on a community that had seen grander days and put their money into the decaying mansion that had what Roger Samuels called, "respectable old bones."

The mansion turned out to be a wise investment. What sold for ninety-five thousand dollars in 1967 was valued today at (depending on which one of Sausalito's ever-gracious but endlessly optimistic real estate agents you asked) fifteen to eighteen million dollars.

Warren Bradley got a thrill by merely driving up to the grand old mansion.

While it was impressive, and while Roger Samuels had left a generous estate that assured Alma's future regardless of the number of years she lived, the care she might require, or the maintenance that the old home might need, there was still a feeling of sadness and obsolescence about the place.

Alma's one child, a daughter who had followed in her father's footsteps and entered the world of business law, was long gone from the house. For many years, Alma had been left on her own to wander from one empty room to another. And although she tried to keep herself busy, the physical burden of her ninety years had begun to weigh heavily upon her.

Only one full-time staff person remained in Alma's employ:

Louise Allen, who over the past thirty-five years had evolved from maid to cook and finally, caretaker. It was Louise's tired smile that greeted Warren when he rang the bell.

"Hello, Louise, how are you today?"

"Fine, Mr. Bradley. Is Ms. Alma expecting you?"

"She is indeed."

"I'll tell her you're here. Go ahead and take a seat in the sunroom."

As Louise departed, Warren paused, as he always did, to breathe in the intoxicating air of old money.

Warren had what he thought of as "acquired comfort." He lived in a small cottage that he purchased from a lonely, childless widow, who died twenty years earlier. Some, less than kind, claimed Warren stole the house out from under her. Perhaps it was a reward for "keeping her warm at night," they speculated. Others decided to ignore the matter entirely.

Being a cautious consumer can make up for a variety of financial shortcomings. Bypassing Sausalito's outrageously expensive grocery stores and various food boutiques in favor of salmon, steaks, and chicken parts purchased at Costco, which provided the essential ingredients for many of Warren's lavishly presented meals, was a wise and painless way to economize. The fifty-mile round trip drive to the northern part of Marin County was a relatively small sacrifice. Warren just made sure to carry his acquisitions into his house in unmarked boxes and discretely dispose of any Costco packaging in a city trash bin, never in his refuse left out weekly for pickup on the curb. As all great gossips know, prying eyes can be found anywhere. Garbage placed at the curb on the night prior to weekly pickup can provide a treasure trove of information.

Warren was standing at one of the room's many windows,

admiring the view of Richardson Bay and imagining how happy he would be to one day inherit this home, when Alma entered, walking cautiously. One of her longest friends, Beatrice Snyder, had recently broken her hip after a fall. Alma was determined to avoid a similar fate and took care in all her movements.

"Alma, my dear, how are you?" Warren asked, as he kissed her offered hand and smiled warmly.

"I'm as well as can be expected," Alma said, as she gave a wan smile in response to Warren's touch before making herself comfortable in an antique wingback chair that appeared to swallow her hole.

Warren marveled at how Alma, while facing the challenges of declining health, managed to summon the strength and interest in every bit of news he was able to bring her. His only conclusion was that Sausalito was her soap opera and she was addicted to the individual storylines of dozens of its players. Therefore, she tolerated Warren as a reliable source for what most others would consider inconsequential news.

Alma believed herself to be gracious by the simple act of inviting Warren into her home. If not for her love of gossip, he would have no place in her presence. Warren sensed this and at his core thought of her as a heartless creature, while keeping a satisfied smile fixed on his face whenever in her presence.

"Now, Warren," she began in the imperious tone he greatly admired, "what's this business about Grant Randolph?"

As he frequently did, Warren spun a tale over a period of ten minutes that would have taken anyone else a few minutes to tell. But since his only currency was information, he was a master at presenting spare facts in the form of an epic story.

"Well, well! I can tell you, Warren; I'm not at all surprised.

That man has a mean streak in him. Beating his wife senseless. Reprehensible. I knew he was not one of us and this proves me right! Just shocking!"

"If I did not know before how awful that man is, I certainly know it now," Warren said with a false look of deep concern.

"I hope you think twice before putting any of this in your newspaper column. You can never be sure what kind of people you're dealing with. For years, we had a better group of individuals moving into Sausalito. Now, I just don't know," the old woman said with a stern expression and a shake of her head. "These young social-climbers are a different breed."

"My dear, I couldn't put it better."

Alma's advice was music to Warren's ears. Sharing his best scoops with many of his column's casual readers seemed like a foolish waste of a story he could dole out in small portions to all of the town's most influential citizens.

He cringed at the thought of living under the same dark cloud as Rob Timmons. Reporting hard news can make you a target—not of physical harm, but of being socially ostracized. A teller of truths that many don't want to hear—and others are enraged to see in print—can be a heavy cross to carry. A newspaper column is instantly available to everyone. On the other hand, whispered gossip allows you to select your listeners.

There was no need for Alma to press this matter. If Randolph could beat his wife, he could easily do physical harm to someone who embarrassed him in print. Still, Warren regretted that he had already concocted the perfect headline:

Arts Commission Chair Grant Randolph Paints an Ugly Picture!

He'd saved it to a file marked *Randolph* in the hope that his cleverly crafted declaration might one day appear above his byline.

The longer Alma thought about the incident, the more agitated she became. After a lengthy silence, she suddenly regretted her initial suggestion. "Well, Warren, what are you going to do about this? It would be an outrage for Randolph to be allowed to stay as chair of the arts commission: a violent man in a distinguished community position? That's unacceptable!"

It quickly occurred to Warren that their conversation was going in the wrong direction. If Alma presumed that he wished to play the combatant, she was mistaken.

Warren paused and uttered an extended, "Well…" which gave the appearance that he was deep in thought. Then he began: "I have eyes and ears everywhere. First, we'll have to see if his unfortunate wife steps forward and files a charge against him. You know, in many cases these battered women don't pursue their tormentors. They let them back into the house and hope to continue their lives together as if nothing happened."

Warren was indeed flying by the seat of his pants. To begin with, he was ignorant as to the extent of Mrs. Randolph's actual injuries. His only knowledge was that the police had been called by one of Randolph's neighbors, who reported a domestic dispute.

When the Sausalito police officers had arrived, Mrs. Randolph was sprawled across the living room floor, and her husband appeared to have been drinking heavily. For all Warren knew, Grant Randolph might have been released hours after arriving at the county jail. While it made for juicy gossip, the entire incident might amount to far more smoke than fire. Unfortunately for Warren, the possibility of an abused wife was something Alma decided she could not ignore.

"There is no way that man should be allowed to continue in his current position," Alma said with increasing conviction. "While I still believe you need to be careful about what you put in your column, you're in the best position to tell other members of the commission, and the community at large, what sort of man they have on the arts commission. This goes beyond simple gossip. As you know, Warren, Sausalito is a small town. We can't do anything about Randolph choosing to live in Sausalito, but we can make certain he doesn't serve in a position of honor and responsibility."

Warren's chest tightened as Alma dug in.

"Eight months from today we hold our annual Fine Arts Gala. To have that man hosting such an important event won't do! I'm sure you agree!"

At this point, Warren could do nothing but agree. Sounding like a commuter chasing a departing Sausalito ferry early on a workday morning, he breathlessly murmured, "Oh, you're right Alma. I should have thought of that!"

Enough silence stood between them that the ever-hovering Louise thought it appropriate to ask if either of them wished for tea.

Alma thanked her but said she was a little tired and planned on taking a nap. She dismissed Louise, then turned her cold blue eyes on Warren—a cue that it was time for him to leave.

He lifted his rumpled self from the comfortable wingback and silently bid farewell.

"Let me know what happens next regarding this terrible business. If Randolph isn't relieved of his post on the commission by the time planning for the gala begins, I'll have to rethink my support of the entire organization." Warren had never heard such resolve in Alma's voice.

As his car journeyed down the steep road leading back to his home, Warren thought about what had just transpired. In his experience, gossip was rarely intended to turn into action. Instead, it was a flavor, like nectarine juice in a red wine sauce. Savored briefly on the tongue and remembered only by its afterglow.

CHAPTER THREE

Rob Timmons' weekly routine would have exhausted most people, but it was a schedule he had grown accustomed to in the years since his purchase of *The Sausalito Standard.*

Historically, this community tabloid newspaper came out weekly, arriving in mailboxes every Wednesday. But a year after buying the paper for a surprisingly small sum from the estate of its founder, Rob struck upon an idea. If he left the newspaper's center twelve pages intact, but put a different four-page "wrap" of local news around each week's edition, he could significantly expand his readership and, more importantly, his value to advertisers. Thereby, as just one example, *The Peninsula Standard,* covering the neighboring towns of Tiburon and Belvedere, arrived every week with specific news stories and social columns like "Belvedere Buzz" and "Tiburon Talk" unique to those towns. Over the next two years, Rob expanded into Mill Valley, and then started a fourth edition in

Ross Valley, which covered the central Marin towns of Ross, San Anselmo, Larkspur, and Corte Madera.

One thing all of these communities had in common was that each held some of the highest family income zip codes in America. Neighborhoods where the listing of a home with a price of one million dollars or less was considered a "fixer-upper."

To the untrained eye, it may have seemed an impossible task for a news organization run by two full-time individuals: Rob, and his full-time editorial assistant/production manager, Holly Cross.

For community news coverage, Rob recruited a host of mostly retired or semi-retired volunteer contributors. The local stories they covered rarely received any attention from one of the Bay Area's major news outlets. Nevertheless, local readers appreciated knowing about road closures or the planned opening of new bike-only lanes, along with the consideration of new taxes and property assessment changes. Each community edition also needed to cover society news such as birthdays, anniversaries, births, graduations, and charitable events. Sylvia Stokes reported on the social scene in Tiburon, Ed Dondero worked Mill Valley, and Cassie Crenshaw covered the towns of Ross Valley.

Although just thirty-seven, Rob's hair was already flecked with gray. That, along with the web of tiny lines edging his watery blue eyes, gave him the appearance of a man several years older.

He'd grown up in Sausalito, the southern-most of the county's web of small towns. His earliest memories centered around the town's annual Fourth of July parade, in which

Robbie (as he was known then) got to sit atop the city's only fire truck alongside his fire chief dad. At one time, the family even had a Dalmatian named Smoke.

Two-thirds of Marin County is dedicated to local, state, or federal parkland, much of which Rob explored on foot as a boy. It was an endless maze of wooded paths, many lined with giant redwoods, and dramatic trails which crisscrossed the coastal headlands and peaked at several hundred feet before sloping down into a canyon, empty river beds, or the Pacific's edge. As teens, Rob and his friends—Eddie included—rode their bikes on the pedestrian paths that connected Sausalito with other Marin towns located in and around iconic Mount Tamalpais. Except for occasional blues and rock concerts in San Francisco's Golden Gate Park that were half music, half outdoor pot parties, Rob and Eddie, like their parents and neighbors, tended to stay on the Marin County side of the Golden Gate Bridge.

Compared to the city's excitement, Rob's hometown had a slow and lazy rhythm in which each day blended quietly into the next. The summer frequently brought the chilly air that settled over much of the San Francisco peninsula from June through September. Most days were idyllically sunny and cool. Winters could occasionally bring heavy rains, but mostly the weather was as benign as the surroundings.

Tranquility was the general rule that marked Sausalito's days and nights—provided you avoided the city's tourist district, which stretched for approximately a mile along a waterfront street called Bridgeway where, during the peak of summer, visitors by car, bus, ferry, and bicycle overwhelmed the small town.

Awed by an idyllic location that combined houses perched on hills above boats bobbing gently in its harbor, with a verdant mountain to the north and sparkling city lights across the azure bay to the south, people who visited or settled in Sausalito found themselves entranced by its beauty. But in time, many of the residents found life in Sausalito maddeningly peaceful and retreated to more vibrant parts of the Bay Area, such as San Francisco, Berkley, Oakland, San Jose, or the rapidly expanding communities collectively known as Silicon Valley.

As an adult, Rob came to appreciate both points of view. Certainly there were more cultural, social, and business opportunities in other parts of the region, but to native Sausalitans or to those who adopted it as their home, its location and natural beauty were hard to resist. Plus, the influx of tourists during the summer and holiday weekends was a constant reminder that this was a special place to live.

Rob married Karin Klein, the daughter of a local family dentist. They settled into a rental on Easterby Street that they both called "the Love Nest." Their son and daughter were born two years apart. By the time the children were enrolled in Sparrow Creek, Sausalito's popular preschool, Rob's parents had retired to a condominium in San Diego and handed Rob and Karin the keys to the family home on Filbert Street.

As far back as Rob could remember, Sausalito was a town filled with colorful characters. The most eccentric were the "houseboat people"—artists and bohemians mostly—who lived in abandoned boats and floating homes tethered along the public docks that once were part of the Marinship boatyards, which boomed in the period of World War II, during the building of the "Liberty Ships" that carried vital supplies for the war effort. Some of these individuals were decades-old fixtures, whereas others just drifted into town for a few months or a few years, and then, just as quietly, moved on.

The steady increase in property values eroded the base of Sausalito's third and fourth generation residents; individuals who could not afford to live in the community they had grown up in. It was not uncommon inside of the two local-serving bars, Smitty's and The No Name, to find one of the remaining children or grandchildren of Sausalito's founding generation of merchants, fisherman, boat builders, and day laborers, assuaging their regrets over selling long-held family property. "Now I've got enough money to pay cash for a nice home out in the East Bay hills," they would announce while buying drinks for friends to celebrate their newfound wealth.

Rob knew that he and Karin might make that same choice in twenty years after their kids were grown and living independent lives. But his real hope was to keep the home in the family, and if possible, live out their years there.

"A lot of people dream about ending up in a place like this," he told Karin one mild star-dusted night after getting their children to sleep. "We're already here. I'd like to travel one day, but after seeing the world, I think I'd be happy to return to Sausalito."

The very first thing Warren did upon coming home from Alma's was to open a fine Madeira. Sipping it, he wondered about his next column. Even he was growing tired of his oft-repeated complaints about careless tourists and inconsiderate teens.

How heroic would he appear if he used his column to make a direct assault on Grant Randolph? At that moment, his cell phone rang.

The caller ID flashed: "Alma S."

He hesitated to push the talk button but knew there was no hope of avoiding Alma. She would track him down within an hour or two.

Quickly, he cleared his throat, slapped a smile on his face, and hit the talk button.

"Yes, hello Alma."

As she often did, Alma ignored pleasantries. "I want you to call Ethel Landau and discuss this situation with her," she barked. "Ethel's been on the arts commission for years and supported Randolph becoming chair of the commission."

Warren's palms dampened as he considered the obvious: This situation was now beyond his control.

Warren was aware that anything you said to either Ethel, or Alma, quickly got back to the other.

"I'll call her right now," Warren promised, hoping to sound positive and cheerful.

"I've been thinking about this since you left my house. This man Randolph could be a black eye to the integrity of every other member serving on the arts commission, including Ethel! You are well aware of my feelings—his continuing presence on the board is unacceptable! After you have filled Ethel in on the details, I'll speak to her as well. Call me back," she barked, and then clicked off.

Warren could not remember Alma this animated since she

organized the effort to prevent outdoor café dining in the city's downtown district.

In fact, when anything that was popular with the town's under-fifty set was voted down by the Sausalito City Council —a body dominated by Councilmember Robin Mitchell for more than a quarter of a century—the Ladies of Liberty were assumed to be the unseen hand behind the effort.

As to chairs and tables on city streets, their unified battle cry became, "Outdoor dining indeed!" In their view, it was just another tactic by realtors, merchants, and restaurateurs to lure tourists to stay and dine and deny locals the quiet enjoyment of their downtown during most spring, summer, and autumn evenings.

Perhaps it was time for Warren to take action on the matter of Randolph. He was, after all, the only one among Alma's inner circle who had a newspaper column delivered weekly into every Sausalito home.

When feeling pressed by unexpected events, Warren would go to his kitchen and make himself a treat. Food preparation gave him time to consider his next step.

To relieve his worries, Warren made himself a crepe, with eggs, milk, vanilla and a half-cup of brandy, topped with apricot jelly and sprinkled with powder sugar.

A half hour later, his outlook on life had brightened. Sipping a cappuccino, he felt empowered to do as Alma had instructed.

He had no concern about building a case against Randolph, but if the ladies were going to ask him to press for Randolph's removal as commission chair, he'd need more than the idle chatter he often spun in his column.

Warren was not naturally given to the life of an investigative reporter: gathering facts, checking and re-checking sources, and digging through files. But Alma was pushing him to lead the effort to expose Randolph and press for his expulsion.

It wouldn't hurt if he came to the battle armed with a few facts.

CHAPTER FOUR

G rant Randolph and his wife, Barbara, had moved to Sausalito less than two years earlier. They were still newcomers in the eyes of their long-established neighbors.

They managed to create a minor buzz upon their arrival. Grant had run a successful art gallery back in New York City and sold it for a handsome profit.

This was a part of his backstory, but certainly not all.

Randolph was a native of Providence, Rhode Island. Degreed at Brown University in art history, he came to New York City during the struggling economy of the early1990s. After two years of working at a long-established Upper East Side gallery, he, along with two equally young and adventure-some partners, made a bold move into the emerging art scene in the lower Manhattan neighborhood of SoHo. The area, south of Houston Street and north of Canal Street, was in transition at the time, with one block showing the promise of a coming new century and another block still suffering from the neglect of the 1960s.

Their gamble turned out to be a wise one. As the city began to emerge from a decade of slow growth, their gallery, The Discerning Eye, became a destination for artists on their way up, and for buyers looking to purchase the art of a select few painters and sculptors with promising futures.

Barbara Stevens came to work as a sales associate for The Discerning Eye just at a time the gallery—thanks to a feature in *The New York Times*—was gaining awareness. She had a newly minted degree in art history from nearby New York University. That, and her twenty-five-year-old body, soon attracted the eager eyes of the then thirty-year-old partner and gallery director, Grant Randolph.

They were both attractive people. Grant had thick, dark, wavy hair, brown eyes, and a sweet smile that, to Barbara, seemed to say, "I'm a lot more dangerous than I look."

And Barbara was a young woman who defined the word "Wow" to her legion of admirers. Her light brown hair was cut short in the style of the times, and her dark green eyes held the stare of anyone who looked her way. In very little time, she became a topic of admiring comments and conversation in the tight circle of New York's art gallery world.

Barbara's carefully presented appearance—proper, but with a hint of mischief—attracted Grant's intellectual and carnal appetites. At the same time, Grant's intelligence, charm, and purposeful demeanor were wildly attractive to Barbara.

Within six months of Barbara's arrival at the gallery, Grant had kicked his Jamaican artist girlfriend to the curb and moved Barbara into his lower-Manhattan condominium. It was in one of a crop of new high rises that offered views of the harbor and the massive twin towers of the World Trade Center.

Years later, on the day before 9/11, Grant begged off an eight o'clock breakfast invitation for the following morning at Windows on the World with a London art broker. He and Barbara had planned to sleep in, take in an exhibit at yet another new SoHo gallery, and then enjoy a leisurely day in celebration of their fifth wedding anniversary.

Because of the double-paned windows that helped soften the din of a city that never sleeps, the Randolphs never heard the plane that crashed into the North Tower at 8:46 AM. But the scream of sirens that began moments later caused both Grant and Barbara to bolt out of bed. They didn't think to turn on the TV until thirty minutes later when they looked on in silent horror as a second plane flew directly into the 80th floor of the South Tower.

"Oh my God!" Grant screamed as Barbara's knees buckled watching the unfolding horror. The South Tower fell first in an explosion of dust that gave it the appearance of an upside down volcanic eruption. Both were staring in stunned silence, mumbling tearfully, "Oh God! Oh God!"

Thirty minutes later, they gasped and held their breaths with the same sense of stunned disbelief as the North Tower collapsed in an equally thunderous roll, releasing a second mushroom cloud of dust that added to the particles of gray powder accumulating on Grant and Barbara's windows.

Barbara wept, tormented by the senseless destruction of human life, a short walk from their home.

Grant remembered as a college student coming down from Providence for a weekend trip to Manhattan. Walking the quiet streets of lower Manhattan on a Sunday when all the bulls and bears of Wall Street had gone home to rest, he looked at the ancient gravestones next to Trinity Church, then walked toward the massive twin towers. They were viewed at that time as grossly out of scale with their surroundings. But over the years, the twin giants became an accepted, if not welcome, part of the landscape of lower Manhattan.

On weekend walks through their Tribeca neighborhood, Grant and Barbara often made it a point to stand at the very foot of one of the twin giants and look straight up while shaking their heads in wonder. Against a deep blue sky, the endless structure of shining steel and glass seemed like a stairway to heaven.

The horror of that day was something neither of them could forget. It was one thing to watch the disaster on television hundreds or thousands of miles away. It was an entirely different experience living so close to ground zero.

For two additional days, they stayed inside their home thinking of nothing else. The gallery remained shut for the balance of the week.

On Friday, they made their first venture outside. Both were prepared with cloth handkerchiefs to place over their mouths and noses, fearing potentially toxic particles that were still floating through the air. Their walk didn't last very long. Seeing people desperate for information, posting pictures anywhere they could of missing friends and loved ones, made the loss of innocent lives all the more overwhelming.

The London gallery owner chose not to dine alone at Windows on the World located on the 102nd floor of the North Tower. It was a fortunate choice; no one in the restaurant at 8:46 that fateful morning survived. The following week, Grant's London friend, now back home, sent him a note that concluded, "I imagine the only reason we're both alive today is that you and Barbara decided to marry on September 11, 1996. I know for certain I will always remember your wedding anniversary!"

In the years after the tragedy the city recovered, but Grant and Barbara never entirely did. The tragedy changed them forever. While not directly in harm's way, the proximity to the event left them both with an odd sense of survivors' guilt. They would never know how many of the tragedy's victims they'd sat next to at a lunch counter, a coffee shop, or passed on the street in the weeks, months and even years before that dark day. The thought of missing neighbors with whom they never thought to exchange a nod, a small smile, or any form of recognition, haunted both of them. Precious souls ignored, anonymous, and now vanished forever.

With each person Randolph watched placing a picture on a door or a lamppost of a loved one, he thought of Barbara doing the same if he had not turned down that breakfast invitation.

Both he and Barbara had always enjoyed casual evening cocktails, but alcohol after that tragic day became a refuge for both of them. A place where they could put life's disappointments aside and find peace in the soft embrace of a stiff drink.

The sentiment, "We're here today and gone tomorrow," they repeated often to each other when hesitating for a moment about mixing that second, or third, cocktail.

As for the gallery and the surrounding area, life went on. Profits soon returned and then kept heading upward—bigger and better than either of them ever imagined.

More than a decade after 9/11, Grant and his partners got an offer to purchase their business that was too outlandish to refuse. Grant, blessed with an uncanny sense of timing, chose as well to sell many of the art pieces he had acquired over the past fifteen years. He sold off all but his personal favorites and parked the profits in a low-risk cash management fund until he and Barbara could decide what to do with their lives.

Unofficially retired and still relatively young, Grant suggested they take a road trip along the California coast. It was May, a perfect time for the two of them to enjoy this picturesque part of America.

In their professional lives, they had visited Los Angeles and San Francisco on several occasions. But neither of them had taken the time to enjoy and explore California's coast. They started at the busy beaches and yacht-filled harbors of San Diego and La Jolla and took all the time they wanted heading north.

They passed the mansions of Montecito and strolled along Stearns Wharf in the town of Santa Barbara. They stopped at the old mission city of San Luis Obispo, and the small coastal town of Los Osos on Morro Bay. They were wowed by the old Hearst Castle in San Simeon and held their breaths as they proceeded along the winding and treacherous curves of Highway 1 between San Simeon and Big Sur.

They stopped at Nepenthe, a restaurant that hugged a cliff south of Carmel, for an early dinner while they took in incredible ocean views from the restaurant's expansive outdoor patio.

After enjoying the adjacent communities of Monterey, Carmel-by-the-Sea, and Pacific Grove, they spent three days on the Sonoma Coast, north of San Francisco. Nearly three weeks into their trip, they parked their car along a deserted two-mile stretch of beach, north of Fort Bragg and south of the small town of Westport, in Mendocino County. Walking barefoot, enjoying a warm sun and a crisp breeze, Grant looked out and caught the unforgettable view of an enormous gray whale breaching out in the blue Pacific, perhaps no more than two hundred yards from the spot where they stood. Less than a minute later, he and Barbara, at the same time, said, "Did you see that—" as a second whale, also traveling south to north, breached as well.

They spread a small blanket and sat down on the dry, warm sand. For nearly an hour, Grant and Barbara held each other while they watched a parade of whales putting on a show just for them. Later, at a bed and breakfast inn they had booked in Westport for their last night on the coast, they learned about what they had seen. "That was a feeding frenzy for krill by a pod of gray whales making their spring migration from Mexico's Baja Peninsula to the Gulf of Alaska," the small hotel's operator explained. "You could wait years to see a show like that. You were just at the right place at the right time."

It was that night, sitting on the porch outside their bedroom, listening to the relentless waves of the Pacific hitting the shore and looking up at a star-covered sky, that the Randolphs decided to leave the East Coast for the West Coast. The next morning at breakfast, their appetites driven by new possibilities, they began planning their move.

They quickly decided that they would look for a home in the Bay Area. But while they had made several visits to San Francisco for studio openings, they didn't know much about the communities around the world-famous city. They resolved to take whatever time they needed to learn about the East Bay, South Bay, and North Bay before making a choice.

Traveling back south to San Francisco along Highway 128, they made several stops at wineries along the Anderson and

Alexander valleys. By the time they reached the Hotel Healdsburg, they had enjoyed one too many tasting rooms along their way. Wisely, they booked the last available room at the upscale hotel, deciding to spend the night before driving any farther.

Shortly after opening the door to their room, both Grant and Barbara flopped down on top of the king-sized bed and fell sound asleep. They woke to the first rays of sunlight coming through the room's heavy drapes, which they had neglected to close entirely. Sitting up on the bed, Grant looked around and gave a long, low whistle.

"Barb, wake up. This has got to be the nicest room I ever woke up in without remembering checking into."

"Jeez, you're right, Grant," Barbara said peeking out of one eye. "I wonder what we spent?"

Neither one of them was pleased when they found out the room cost nine hundred dollars for the night.

"I guess it's cheaper than a DUI, and all the headaches the car rental company would have put us through if I'd run over a deer while driving the back roads of Napa County," Grant offered.

"And, God, what beautiful country this is!" Barbara added. "Not to mention all the great wines!"

"Maybe we could be happy living here?" Grant wondered aloud.

"I think 70 miles north of San Francisco is a little too far for you to be from a major city. You may love fresh air and vineyards, but you've got steel, glass, and concrete in your veins," Barbara said with a laugh.

"You're right, but there's something to be said for finding a little more peace in our lives."

"I agree, darling. But too much peace, and I could see you losing your mind."

I t was still early when they stepped out to meet the day, discovering, thankfully, that they were at least sober enough to have parked their car in a legal space.

They wandered every street around Healdsburg's charming town square and found the perfect place for a relaxing breakfast.

They fell into a conversation with the couple sitting at the two-top table ten inches away from their own. Patrons of the popular eatery happily sacrificed some extra space and greater privacy for the efficient service and excellent food.

Between generous cappuccinos, yummy omelets, and homemade biscuits, they got to know the couple seated next to them: Ray and Debbie Sirica, who they learned had relocated to Sausalito from their native Chicago ten years earlier.

"Some of the locals can be a little quirky," they explained, but they both agreed that the town was a great place to live. "It's a quick trip into San Francisco, but none of the hassles of life in a big city," Ray announced with a smile.

Grant reasoned that Ray—a big man, tall, broad-shouldered, with big hands, and a large frame to match—was five or so years older than himself. Debbie was closer to Ray in age than Barbara was to Grant. She was slim, with a pleasant, smiling face. Her hair was tinted to cover its emerging gray, and her brown eyes never wavered in their focus. Her manner was kind, and cautiously sincere.

Grant dealt with a lot of personalities in gallery sales. He had convinced himself over time that he was a reasonably sound judge of character. Ray was one of those rare people, who from the moment you met seemed like someone you had known for years. His relaxed smile said, "What you see is who I am." There was trustworthiness in his open manner. It was a quality that Grant took a liking to instantly.

Both of the Randolphs felt comfortable enough with the Siricas to exchange contact information. Before they went their separate ways, Ray and Debbie asked if they would be in Sausalito on Friday night. "If so, come and join us for a reception we're holding for the city's fine arts commission," Ray suggested, and added, "Given your backgrounds, they're all people I think you'll enjoy meeting."

An hour later, as Grant and Barbara began the nearly two-hour ride south to San Francisco, he and Barbara agreed that Sausalito, a town they knew of but had never spent any time in, might indeed be the perfect spot to begin their new and hopefully happier future.

CHAPTER FIVE

To both Barbara and Grant, Sausalito seemed to answer many of the desires they had difficulty verbalizing when they first imagined moving to California.

For starters, like their new friends and former Chicago natives, the Siricas, they would be putting bone-chilling winters and uncomfortably hot summers behind them.

After settling into their room in Sausalito's Casa Madrona Hotel, the Randolphs reached out to the Siricas and invited them to dinner at Poggio, the popular trattoria adjacent to the hotel.

The afternoon before their dinner engagement, the Randolphs took a leisurely stroll along the Sausalito marina, which held seemingly endless rows of piers lined with motor yachts and sailing sloops. Turning south, they walked past the small tourist district, busy as usual with day visitors. Farther along, they strolled the south end of Bridgeway, which hugs the bay until it winds its way up towards the Marin Headlands and onto the Golden Gate Bridge.

The tourist district itself lasts less than a mile. Where it ends, the Randolphs found themselves in a quiet, quaint setting of mostly small to moderately sized homes. They were mesmerized by the houses stacked on hills. In the soft blue air and bright light of a May afternoon, it could have been a painting of a small, seaside Mediterranean village.

"It's a little too perfect to be real, don't you think?" Grant said to Barbara as they began walking up a steep path.

They turned right onto Third Street, which was an even steeper incline that leads to a small neighborhood park called Southview. There, they sat down on a bench to recover from a climb neither was accustomed to making. From there, they looked out on a vista that included the San Francisco skyline, the Bay Bridge, and the golden hills of Berkeley, and Oakland beyond. They could even see the clock tower at the center of the Berkeley campus. Closer to them was Angel Island and the Belvedere/Tiburon Peninsula. Sitting in the middle of the bay was iconic Alcatraz Island, home of the long-closed infamous prison, known simply as "The Rock."

Barbara leaned her head comfortably into Grant's shoulder as he pulled her in close. "It's lovely, isn't it?"

"You have to keep reminding yourself that it's real! It looks so much like a painting," Grant said.

"It's incredible that we're the only ones sitting up here. If there was a public space in Manhattan with views like these, it would be packed with people. I guess the uphill climb scares off most of the tourists."

"You're right, Barb," Grant said, as he lifted his head to look all around. "I'll need time adjusting to this much quiet."

After years of living and working in lower Manhattan, noise—particularly car horns—was so relentless, one only noticed when it all vanished as it did in the days after 9/11.

"You're right. I don't hear anything right now," Barbara admitted. "No people rushing, no street vendors, no fire engines, or police sirens. This much quiet is a little unsettling, don't you think?"

Grant gave a short laugh, and after a long pause said, "Certainly nothing we're accustomed to. But I think I could grow to love this kind of peace and quiet."

Barbara snuggled in and reached up to her husband's lips to share a kiss.

"Does it make you happy, darling?" he asked.

Barbara thought for a moment, and said, "It does. I'm ready for a little solitude and sanity in our lives."

"I think we both are!"

A t dinner that night, Debbie and Ray shared with the Randolphs how they came to settle in Sausalito.

"I took over my father's business. He made high-end nightwear—pajamas, nightgowns, and so on," Ray explained. "A couple of years ago, we were approached by a big manufacturer in the business. They made us an offer to buy the entire operation that, as my dad was fond of saying, knocked our socks off. So, we took the money, and started to ask ourselves, 'What now? We can live wherever we want, so where would that be?' In a lot of ways, Chicago is a great town. But to be honest with you, the weather is less than ideal, way too hot in the summer and way too cold in the winter."

"Florida and Arizona don't have the feel of Northern California. In places like Phoenix and Orlando, you see a lot more of concrete, cars, and buildings, then you see of nature," Debbie added. "We always stayed a few extra days when a trade show brought us out to San Francisco. On days off, we would often take the ferry over to Sausalito, which is less than a thirty-minute ride. We just fell in love with this little town! So, when we had the chance to reinvent our lives, we started looking into home prices in the area. We bought after the tech bubble burst. It wasn't cheap, but prices have gone up a lot since."

"It's a good investment," Ray insisted. "Property values around here do one of two things. They stay flat for a year or two, or they go up."

The following day, Barbara and Grant rented bicycles across the street from their hotel and rode north along the waterfront into the charming town of Mill Valley, where the bike trail ended at a plaza called the Mill Valley Depot. It was once the endpoint of the Northwestern Pacific Railroad's Marin County Interurban electric train service, which came to an end shortly after the opening of the Golden Gate Bridge in 1937. Today the depot served as a coffee and bookshop surrounded by high-end boutiques.

After chaining their bikes to a rack at the edge of the plaza, they purchased sandwiches and drinks and walked the few city blocks up to Old Mill Park, where they sat at a picnic table in the middle of a grove of massive redwood trees.

Later, while biking the same path back to Sausalito, they

discussed their day and agreed that in the picture book town of Mill Valley, they had found one more reason to believe that Southern Marin County was the perfect choice for them.

That night, they took the short drive from their hotel to the Sirica home on Sausalito Boulevard. It was their first time driving through the town's winding hills. Steep, narrow lanes with blind curves can be a little intimidating to someone driving along them for the first time, but finding beautiful bay vistas around every bend more than made up for the discomforting feeling of learning to navigate their way through this unfamiliar terrain.

For a couple accustomed to the opulent homes of their multi-millionaire art collector clients, the Randolphs were still impressed by the Siricas' home.

"Looks like the cover of *Architectural Digest,*" Barbara said quietly to Grant, as they walked up the steps to the front door.

"Why are you whispering?" Grant asked.

"I've heard people in small towns have big ears."

"You're silly," Grant said teasingly, yet also in a soft voice.

Grant and Barbara were greeted warmly by Ray and Debbie. None of the other guests had arrived yet, prompting Grant to ask if they had come too early.

Ray laughed. "No problem, happy to see you guys. Let's get you both a drink."

Their early arrival gave the Siricas time to walk the Randolphs around the property.

As they stepped out onto the veranda and into a soft early

evening breeze, they admired postcard-worthy views of the bay and the surrounding tree-covered hills. The Randolphs were once again impressed by the beauty of what they already thought of as their new corner of the world.

"You can see why we fell in love with this property," Debbie said.

"It's just stunning, both the house and the view," Barbara replied.

Once the thirty or so other guests arrived, everyone seemed interested in Barbara and Grant's story: how they met, their experience owning and operating a Manhattan art gallery, the tragic events of 9/11, and Grant's good fortune in missing that breakfast engagement atop the World Trade Center.

Ethel Landau, who detailed her longtime service on the city's arts commission, was not shy in pressing Grant to get involved with her group. As they spoke, Warren Bradley—ever watchful, particularly of newcomers—paid careful attention.

"If you do settle here, I want you to attend an arts commission meeting and find out what our group is all about," Ethel said.

"I'd enjoy that," Grant responded enthusiastically.

"Sausalito has an incredible history with the arts. I think you'll be impressed."

Grant nodded. "In fact, I've been reading up on it. Jean Varda, Shel Silverstein, Gordon Onslow—all renowned! It would have been fun to be part of the arts community back then."

"Show off," Warren muttered to himself, growing increasingly jealous of this handsome and apparently successful man. He knew that two of the five commission seats were up in less than a year. One of the commissioners had already made clear his intention to step down. Warren had his eye on that position. Now, it looked as if he'd have to compete for it with this newcomer.

Maybe he'll let loose with some tidbit that I can use to disqualify him, Warren thought hopefully.

He waited an hour, then walked over to Grant and introduced himself. "I understand that you and your wife are thinking of moving to our fair city," Warren began with a deceptively welcoming smile.

"That's right," Grant replied.

"You know, we're a very tight-knit little community. Some people find it difficult to fit in."

"Where I come from, people are more aggressive. In a place as big and as busy as Manhattan there's no sense waiting for an invitation. You make space for yourself at the table."

"It's very different here," Warren insisted. "We look out for our neighbors. We stay close. Probably, some would say, too close."

"I think every place takes some getting used to," Grant countered, sensing an instinctive dislike for Warren.

"I'm sure you'll do fine as long as you remember that people think you should be here ten years or more before you play an active role in the community. I guess we're just old-fashioned that way. By the way, did you try some of my bruschetta with white beans, tomatoes, and olives?"

Grant held up a hand. "Thanks, but I'll pass. Now if you'll excuse me, I see my wife trying to wave me over."

How dare he, Warren fumed silently. Not even an attempt to be gracious!

At that moment Warren vowed one day he would take Grant Randolph down a peg or two.

L ater that night, when they were back in their hotel room, Grant said, "Barbara, thanks again for saving me from that creepy guy—you know, the one who thinks he's a gourmet chef."

Barbara shook her head. "You should have seen his face when you passed on his appetizer. Talk about taking it personally! You know, Grant, you could have told him you're gluten sensitive. Oh, by the way, Warren writes for the local paper —*The Sausalito Standard.*"

Grant rolled his eyes. "Let me guess: restaurant reviews."

"I hear it's more like a gossip column." Barbara laughed. "Based on the look on his face when you turned down his bruschetta, I wouldn't be surprised if you've made your first enemy in town."

"He did say he wanted to interview us for the paper after we settle into town, but that was before I made him cry over his bruschetta." Grant shrugged. "I don't know what we would tell him for his ridiculous column. Frankly, I got the feeling that he's little more than an old busybody."

"He seemed harmless enough to me," Barbara replied.

"I guess Ray and Debbie are right when they say that this place is just an overgrown village with a cast of different characters. I'm just wondering if it might get a little claustrophobic."

"Anytime we want, there's a big city called San Francisco

just thirty minutes away by ferry, and even faster most times by car, that we can go visit."

"You're right," Grant said as his mouth relaxed into a smile. "Sausalito will certainly be a major change from Manhattan. I hope we won't miss living in a place where hardly anyone knows your name."

CHAPTER SIX

J ust four months after their first introduction to Sausalito, Barbara and Grant pulled into the driveway of their new home. It wasn't the Siricas' mini-mansion, but it was probably the best three-bedroom cottage under two million dollars in Sausalito. Between the sale of their Manhattan condominium and the money from their share of the gallery, they still had a significant amount of savings, allowing them to live in comfort whether choosing to work or not.

Grant and Barbara did not doubt that they would re-engage with the world of fine art at some point. But for now, they wanted to focus on establishing a new life in an entirely different place.

As Grant soon discovered, all of his unspent energy, once invested in the daily pressure of life in New York and the challenge of staying ahead in the highly competitive world of fine art sales, now required a new outlet. Picking out fabric swatches and comparing paint chips as they tinkered with every room of their new home was not going to hold his interest for very long.

One afternoon, while out for a walk with Ray, Grant shared with him that he loved his new home and his new surroundings. "But I'm itching to burn off some excess energy."

"Been there, done that," Ray said without hesitation. "Why don't we join a gym? We could both benefit from a little honest sweat. All this good living is turning me into a pile of mush."

"If I remember correctly, there's a gym near the Sausalito houseboat docks," Grant suggested.

Ray shook his head. "Nah. The place is 90% aerobics machines; it doesn't feel like a real gym to me if I'm sitting on a stationary bike or jogging on a treadmill."

"What do you mean by 'a real gym'?"

"I was a starting defensive center on my high school's varsity football team," Ray explained. "Except for the last few years, I've worked out regularly since I was fifteen. I'll know the right gym when I see it."

When they stepped inside of Gold's Gym, near the town of Corte Madera about 10 miles north of Sausalito, Ray knew they had found the right place.

To begin with, it smelled like a gym. As they strolled through the cavernous space that had once served as a distribution warehouse, Ray was impressed at the three different areas dedicated to strength resistance training. From racks of free weights to dozens of pulley-operated weight machines, they both liked what they saw.

And when one of the gym's fitness associates told them that the monthly membership was thirty-five dollars with no initial membership fee other than an upfront charge for the first month, they looked at each other, smiled, and signed on the dotted line.

On the short drive south to Sausalito, Ray talked excitedly about their new gym. In fact, it was all he could talk about, starting with, "Thirty-five bucks! Debbie spends more than that getting her nails done every week."

"I've never been much of a gym guy, but I've got to admit I'm excited."

"Buddy, you'll see what a big difference this is going to make! Look, Grant, we're both getting to the age where we begin that long slide toward falling apart. If we don't do something now to slow that process, we'll be beyond hope in another ten years. In your twenties, you can coast, you should start paying attention in your thirties, and if you're not doing something to improve your body in your forties, it all starts to show."

"Ray, you're right. I enjoy the good life. But cocktails, appetizers, steaks, and dessert while sitting out on your deck admiring the view are not going to get me back into the shape I was once in."

"We'll be a little sore the first couple of weeks, but believe me, you're going to see some real changes over the next few months, and you're going to like what you see."

Grant did indeed like the results he saw within a few weeks. He particularly noticed the way Barbara ran her nails across his chest after he showered and walked into the bedroom with only a towel wrapped around his tightening waistline. While he didn't tell her, he was proud that she was noticing his progress.

Two months into what Ray referred to as his "Sirica boot camp program," the changes were becoming even more noticeable. Grant's body frequently balked at the demands he was putting upon it, but the increased passion of his and Barbara's lovemaking more than compensated for a strain here and a little soreness there.

It had been a long time since Grant had caught Barbara looking at him longingly. This subtle but noticeable change in her increased his commitment to Ray's rigorous workout program.

Ray admitted that he, too, had seen a change in Debbie. "She hasn't shown this much interest in me, physically I mean, since we were both twenty-somethings. It's nice getting some of that back."

The Randolph's cottage was in excellent condition, but it needed a lot of attention before Barbara and Grant would be genuinely pleased with its appearance. For starters, there was the hideous wallpaper in both the dining room and living room that had to go. The bedrooms, painted in soft shades of beige, probably a wise choice for a seller seeking to provide muted tones so as not to distract prospective buyers, was not to the Randolphs' liking. Both of them believed that color gave a room life and personality.

"And," as Barbara noted, going from room to room with Grant, "there are so many small changes that could make a big difference, like crown molding throughout, new windows, and new window treatments."

It wasn't their initial intention to sink more money into what was already an expensive home, but it was hard to resist.

"A home with world-class views, in an unquestionably beautiful setting, should present itself to the world with the tasteful touches it deserves," Barbara reasoned.

In the evenings they sat on the high terrace holding cocktails and continued their enjoyment of sweeping bay panoramas. Ray had cautioned, "For the first six months, the views make it hard to turn away. Thank goodness it becomes less hypnotic after you've lived in your place for awhile."

After much loving attention, Grant and Barbara created the look they had envisioned the first day they walked through the property.

It was time for both of them to look for other interests.

Barbara and Grant continued to enjoy Ray and Debbie's company. And yet, after one more evening of hearing Ray talk about how you decide when to drop one nightwear designer and go with another, both of them decided it was time to widen their circle of friends.

To that end, Barbara happily accepted an invitation to a meet and greet luncheon at the Sausalito Women's League. That same day, Grant committed to attending a meeting of the Sausalito Fine Arts Commission.

The Women's League gathering was held in a century-old building that was an estate gift from the league's founder, Dorothy Landau. Her granddaughter, Ethel Landau, spoke of her predecessor in reverential terms. She also gave Barbara a comprehensive history of the league.

A light luncheon was served with a mixed fruit cobbler for dessert prepared by, as Alma Samuels proudly announced, "Sausalito's master chef, Warren Bradley."

During this friendly but rather staid event, as Barbara later detailed for Grant, most of the conversation centered around an annual program called the Winter Follies, a holiday season satirical musical review of life in Sausalito.

Ethel shared a photo album of previous follies with Barbara and three other potential new members. Pointing to a chorus line of women with red cheeks and red noses, she explained that first year members are expected to join the "reindeer chorus." Barbara smiled but was horrified by pictures of giggling women in ridiculous outfits.

Warren made a point of sitting next to Barbara for a brief time and told her how impressed he was with both she and her husband. But after those few moments, she thought that Grant was quite right in suggesting that something was off-putting about Sausalito's gregarious gourmet.

Because Ray and Grant could not get in their usual morning workout, Grant was not home when Barbara came back from her early afternoon luncheon. Later, when Grant arrived, he rushed to take a shower and head out for the arts commission meeting that, to Grant's way of thinking, began much too early: six o'clock.

The meeting took place at the senior center, located on the lower level of city hall. It had just started when Grant entered and quickly took a seat. The members of the commission sat at a long, narrow conference table facing five rows of chairs, seven seats across, nearly all of which were empty. In fact, there was one more commissioner (five) than attendees (four).

With such a small gathering, the commission's elderly chairperson, Arthur Bingham, stopped to introduce himself and the other members of the committee to this first-time attendee. Ethel proudly exclaimed to her fellow commissioners, "Grant has an impressive background in fine arts, and I hope he will be a regular attendee at future meetings."

"Please stay for refreshments after the meeting, so we can all get to know you better," Bingham said to Grant. "We have a mixed fruit cobbler generously prepared by Sausalito's gracious gourmet, Warren Bradley."

Grant turned to his right to find the outstretched hand of that frumpish man with the unruly mustache. Grant smiled, nodded, and shook Warren's hand. With pleasant smiles exchanged, both men turned back toward the commission, who all nodded politely in return.

The two other guests were there to present proposed agreements for tent rentals and catering services for the annual art gala. By the meeting's conclusion, only Warren and Grant remained as guests.

Ethel took Grant aside. In a soft murmur, she divulged, "Sadly, Arthur Bingham wishes to leave the commission after his term expires. Please consider getting involved! We need some young blood in the mix, and you've got the credentials to make a marvelous addition to the commission."

Warren did not appreciate what he heard from a discreet distance.

With all the cobblers I've prepared for this group, I should be the next commission member! Regardless of hurt feelings, Warren reminded himself to smile as he suggested to Grant that he help himself to some cobbler. Grant's refusal, patting his flat abs and saying that he had not yet had dinner, was one more mark against this apparent social climber.

Back home, as Grant and Barbara talked over cocktails, they quickly realized that they had both come away from their social interactions with differing points of view.

"After seeing the Sausalito Women's League in action, it's just too silly for me," Barbara sighed.

Grant shrugged. His meeting had left him considering the commission's future potential. "The commission is well-intentioned, and they have an idea of what they want to do. They need a little help getting there."

"What are they hoping to accomplish?"

"They see their mission as bringing greater attention to the fine arts that are already here in Sausalito and Southern Marin.

They have a history that runs pretty deep. There's an old marine warehouse at the north end of town that provides studio space to twenty plus local artists I've heard about it, but never gave it much thought until tonight."

"I'm surprised your radar for emerging talent didn't lead you there before now."

"I think I switched it off, at least as it pertains to the marketing and sale of fine art."

"Well, I think it's grand that you would like to get involved," Barbara said, with what he thought sounded like a hint of disappointment in her voice.

"We could get involved together. There's certainly a lot to be done."

"I'll think about it, Grant. Your favorite part of the business was always cultivation of emerging artists. What I enjoyed was *client* cultivation—bringing art lovers and artists together. And even better, introducing people of means to the world of collecting fine art."

"Sweetheart, any time you want to look at some of the galleries in San Francisco, to either work at or to be an independent rep for, I'm entirely supportive of you doing that."

Barbara smiled, kissed Grant on the cheek, and then passed her hand over his chest. "Wow, these pecs of yours are getting harder by the week!" She moved her index finger around his shoulders and down his increasingly powerful arms. "All of this fresh air must agree with you. You're turning into a beast."

"I don't think it's the fresh air. It's Ray, kicking my butt every time I try to slack off on my workouts."

"Well, I like the results." Barbara pulled Grant closer and kissed him deeply. "A girl could get carried away by a guy like you."

Inspired by her admiration, Grant bent down wrapped his arms around her and lifted her off the ground.

Barbara, in jest, slapped his back and said, "Put me down, you brute."

"Tarzan like Jane. Take Jane to tree house."

"Alright, but remember, be gentle…well, not too gentle."

CHAPTER SEVEN

One month after he attended his first meeting, Grant was formally invited to apply for Arthur Bingham's seat on the arts commission.

After hearing that Ethel had reached out to Grant, Warren chose not to apply.

Grant, unopposed, was selected with little discussion. The other commissioners suggested that Ethel reclaim her previous role as the commission's chair.

To the surprise of everyone, Ethel said, "I'd like to nominate Grant Randolph as our chair. I think he's superbly qualified and would bring a new level of energy to all our efforts."

The other three commissioners, who had long grown weary of the demands of serving on the commission, happily deferred to Ethel's suggestion.

To the surprise of everyone in the room, Grant suddenly found himself the new chair of the Sausalito Fine Arts Commission.

It was an all but unheard of ascension, considering that he

was a relative newcomer to Sausalito and had not previously served on any commission. However, of the many board and commission positions sought after by the town's residents, service on the arts commission was near the bottom of a basket of political plums. A star turn one night during the annual Fine Arts Commission Gala was a poor trade-off for a year's worth of twice-monthly meetings.

Warren repeated Ethel's comments and praise for Grant in his column that week, gritting his teeth with each sentence he wrote. He had to satisfy himself with the thought that the man he now thought of as "pretty boy" would one day fall from the lofty pedestal that Ethel Landau had unwisely placed him upon.

Warren never imagined how soon that fall would come.

To Barbara's amazement, Grant warmed to his role on the commission.

His favorite part was meeting the promising young artists who made up the Sausalito's Gate Six Artists' Cooperative, all of whom he encouraged to apply for his new program of funding artists in residence.

Meanwhile, Barbara had to come up with an acceptable excuse for ducking the offer to join the Sausalito Women's League. When Marilyn Williams, one of Alma Samuels' lieutenants and a charter member of the Ladies of Liberty, eventually did call, Barbara was prepared to be utterly charming—and completely dishonest.

"Oh, Marilyn, this is so sweet of you! Yes, I had so much fun at the luncheon. But since I last saw you, I've accepted a position with the Moss Gallery on Post Street, in San Francisco."

Marilyn sounded like she was getting ready to say something, so Barbara kept speaking.

"I've been so busy settling into my new job and adjusting to the daily commute I just haven't had time to think. I should have reached out to you first. I hope the invitation to the club will remain open so I may reapply when things at my job settle down."

"Oh, absolutely, my dear," Marilyn assured her, but her tone hinted at a level of unspoken disappointment. "Just let me know. And I do have to tell you that I've heard so many good things about your husband Grant's work with the arts commission. He's making quite a name for himself with all the right people."

Barbara hummed and purred her way through the rest of the conversation. During her time in town, she'd learned that warm, welcoming smiles could turn into disapproving frowns with a single misstep. Turning down the invitation to join the league was pushing the envelope for anyone who wanted to remain on the right side of those considered individuals of note. Even though it was small when compared to their lower Manhattan social set, neither of the Grants appreciated being viewed as social outcasts, regardless of the arena they were playing in.

As for the position at the Moss Gallery on San Francisco's Post Street, Barbara's story was something of an embellishment. The Moss Gallery was considered by most aficionados to be the city's leader in both the purchase and sale of works by Northern California's diverse body of established and emerging artists. Just two days earlier, Barbara had interviewed for the position of sales associate with Anna Ruth Moss, the gallery's seventy-two-year-old founder. Given her years of previous experience in the nation's most competitive fine arts acquisition market, more than likely the position could be Barbara's for the asking. What had been a convenient excuse to avoid the vacuous delights of the Sausalito Women's League was a reasonable professional step forward.

Anna Ruth Moss was delighted to hear that Barbara Randolph wished to join her team. Barbara was equally delighted that she would be reconnecting with the art world from a west coast perspective.

Best of all, three days a week she would once again be surrounded by the vitality of a great city. She missed Manhattan more than she ever imagined she would. While San Francisco and New York were as different as Paris and London, it was that buzzing rhythm of a busy city center that gave Barbara the feeling of being back home. Besides, there was something charming about replacing the sound of Manhattan car horns with the chime of ringing bells on cable cars as they went up and down along Powell Street, just steps from the location of the gallery.

Grant was pleased with Barbara's selection of galleries, yet found himself asking repeatedly, "But you are happy with our choice to settle in Sausalito as opposed to San Francisco?"

"Oh, absolutely, Grant. I can't imagine a more idyllic place to live. But I do miss the gallery business, and I need to get back to something that challenges me to be my best. I'll be forty-one in a few months, and that's a little young for retirement," she said with a smile.

"Well, I'm just a little older. You don't think of me as retired, do you?"

"Not exactly…"

Grant frowned. "Okay, maybe in a sense I am, but I'm at least keeping busy."

Barbara came close to saying something else but held back. While Grant was undoubtedly in the best physical shape she had ever seen him in, the competitive business of fine art acquisition and sales had kept him sharp in ways that he was not anymore. There had always been a hungry look in his eyes whenever he was going to make a significant acquisition, knowing that he had several buyers who would eagerly compete against each other to add a particular piece to their collection. That hunger seemed to have vanished.

On some level, Grant knew this truth as well. It was the likely reason he had embraced his involvement in the city's small but thriving art scene.

It was a discussion about their future that neither Barbara nor Grant was willing to have. With the passage of time, Barbara wondered if Grant loved their new life too much.

Grant thought perhaps Barbara did not love it enough.

CHAPTER EIGHT

Warren made it his mission to keep a careful eye on both Barbara and Grant.

His seemingly innocent patter would go something like this: "Have you met the Randolphs? They bought the old McFadden home, up on Bulkley. They seem very nice. I've heard that he ran an art gallery in Manhattan. In fact, Grant Randolph has become chair of the arts commission. I understand he has some exciting new ideas."

Warren would seed a conversation the way farmers pay to seed a cloud—drop enough random thoughts, and you may be delighted to find that it's raining down information.

Most of his prodding would go nowhere. But there were those unexpected moments when a small investment in time led to an unanticipated reward.

"I don't know if I much care for Barbara Randolph," Marilyn Williams said. "We invited her to a lovely luncheon at the league, but then she turned our offer of membership."

"That wasn't very nice of her," Warren said sympathetically. "Did she tell you why she wasn't interested in membership?"

"Something about starting a new job in the city at a place called the Moss Gallery."

"Oh, I've heard of it. Anna Ruth Moss is the owner. She's one of the grand dames of San Francisco's Presidio Heights."

Few things raised the ire of the Ladies of Liberty more than the mention of a Bay Area neighborhood with even more expensive real estate than that of Sausalito.

Warren was a walking directory of the Bay Area's wealthiest and most influential citizens.

"Well, she won't be getting a second invitation to join the league anytime soon! I can tell you that, Warren!"

"I should say."

Bradley begged off Marilyn's invitation for tea. In a few moments, he was on his way. He knew that their exchange might have appeared meaningless, but to an astute observer, it was clear that Barbara was not far from being regarded as a social outcast. That would most likely be a great disappointment to a woman who had hopes of fitting into Sausalito's social circle.

Warren could exploit the tone of these conversations with the highly trained ear of a noted symphony's first violist. It wasn't long before the first small rock he tossed in the water began to ripple back towards him.

Bea confided to Warren: "I've heard some discouraging comments about Barbara Randolph. Frankly, I don't know if that New York gal fits in well with the rest of the community."

Even Alma joined the chorus, telling Warren, "I have my doubts that Barbara Randolph is one of us."

Before writing his "Heard About Town" column the next morning, Warren sat in his small kitchen sipping a cappuccino and wondering how he could stir up trouble for the Grants. Barbara was standing on a social precipice. Surely, there must be some way to give her a little push!

Of course, he reasoned, his column would once again have to serve as his most valuable asset.

He reached Barbara by phone at the gallery. Warren introduced himself and explained, "I want to do a small piece for my column in *The Sausalito Standard* about your new position at the Moss Gallery."

Barbara was pleased to have something in the local paper alerting wealthy collectors that she was affiliated with one of San Francisco's premier galleries.

Near the end of the conversation, she was somewhat surprised when Warren said, "I understand that you recently turned down an invitation to join the league."

"Oh, yes," she responded cautiously. "I'd love to have the time to do it all, but at my age, I have to place my career above social engagements."

Hearing the comment he was looking for, Warren graciously expressed his deepest thanks, wished her the best of luck in her new job, and hurried off the phone. Barbara was equally pleased to have had the opportunity to tell potential clients that she was a dedicated professional.

When Barbara pulled *The Standard* from her mailbox two days later, she turned quickly to Warren's column and found this small item:
"Barbara Randolph, who recently declined an invitation to join the Sausalito Women's League, has accepted a position with the Moss Gallery in San Francisco as a new sales associate. She describes herself as excited to be a part of the gallery's team. As for the league, Mrs. Grant explained, 'At my age, I have to place my career above social engagements.'"

Warren then quoted Marilyn Williams, the Women's League membership chair, about the nature of the league's efforts at community outreach: "I'm sorry to hear that Barbara Randolph considers the league to be little more than a 'social engagement.' In our annual student scholarship drive, and in so many other ways, the league is an essential part of what makes Sausalito, Sausalito!"

Barbara was stunned by the way the piece read. She toyed with the thought that Warren had set her up. Certainly, the article cast her in a negative light. But, after further thought, she was determined to disregard the entire matter. It was merely the small-minded behavior of a person who eats, lives, and breathes small town priorities.

Warren relished his handiwork. Using a light and supposedly innocent touch, he had dealt Barbara Randolph's social standing a terrible blow. As many of Warren's cookbooks instructed, "Spiced properly, it should leave a distinct flavor without creating an overwhelming presence."

That same afternoon Rob sat at his desk and read the entire edition of *The Sausalito Standard*—something, he realized, he did not do often enough. After reading the "Heard About Town" column, Rob barked to Holly to come into his office.

"Do you think this guy Warren Bradley is being a bit of an ass about this woman Barbara Randolph? He pretty much pushes her overboard in his column!"

"What planet have you been living on?" Holly asked with a curious smile and a slight shake of her head. "That's always been Warren's style. Some of the people in this town act like the 'cool kids in school.' They can never feel good about themselves unless they know they have caused someone else to feel bad. Rob, I'm telling ya, if I were you, I'd dump his ass."

"I've thought about it," Rob admitted. "But then Alma and her gang would be organizing another advertiser boycott of *The Standard*, and I've got enough on my plate to deal with without that."

"At least have a talk with Bradley about these hatchet jobs. I'm sure this woman, Barbara, is wondering what she did to have him set her up like this."

During his walk home that evening, Warren's gossip column kept crossing Rob's mind. In truth, he would happily toss Warren out of the paper's circle of community reporters, but he knew that would equal a loss of readership and eventually a loss of ad sales, neither of which *The Standard* could afford. He resolved to leave the status quo for now but made a promise to himself to monitor Warren's column more carefully. He'd start by reading it before putting it on press, and when possible, edit out comments he thought were inappropriate.

Barbara remained willfully unaware that her social standing was quickly eroding. But one day, several weeks after Warren's column about her had appeared, she went for a Saturday afternoon walk with Debbie Sirica and heard for the first time that she was not well thought of by many of the women in town.

Debbie, who had been a longtime member of the league—in fact, she was a former chair of the holiday follies program—seemed shaken by this. "I was surprised to hear many of the women in the league referring to you as the 'ice queen.' When I asked them what they meant by that the only answer I got back was, 'Well, actually, I didn't say that, someone else told me.'"

Further, when Debbie asked them to recall who they heard that from, she was told, "I really can't remember," which Debbie took to mean, "I don't want to talk about this anymore; it's not my problem."

Debbie was annoyed by all this nonsense. But, as she shared with Barbara, "I think they don't like the fact that you're a professional woman with more on your mind than holiday follies, cake sales, and silly gossip."

To Warren's view, damaging Barbara's social standing was the low hanging fruit. He was certain that greater care would need to be taken in what was written about her husband.

It was difficult to control his urge to undermine Grant's standing in town. As much as he prided himself on knowing all there was to know about fine food, music, and art, he was still envious. Warren could never hope to compete with either of the Randolphs' credentials in the art world.

This was made clear during the arts commission's outing to San Francisco's Legion of Honor to see the well-reviewed retrospective of the Danish-French impressionist Camille Pissarro. It was natural for the group to direct their questions to Grant—especially after he corrected Warren's faux pas in confusing Manet with Matisse.

Another time, he corrected Warren, insisting, "No, that's not a work by the American master John Singer Sargent. It's the work of Anders Zorn, arguably Sweden's greatest painter."

Catching the sly smiles of the others, Warren realized that his unquestioned position as a gentleman of culture and refinement was suddenly in doubt.

Making matters worse, Grant had a physique envied by men and admired by women. His fitted shirt did little to hide his flat stomach, broad chest, and massive shoulders—all of which fueled Warren's growing resentment.

Warren's one hope of dismantling this living statue of a man was that Alma and her Ladies of Liberty would in time believe that Grant was just as much of an outsider as his unappreciative wife. He enjoyed speculating with Robin Mitchell that perhaps the two of them were involved in the sale of forged artworks or other nefarious crimes.

"What a delicious scandal that would be," Warren told her, as his gray eyes lit up and his aging face broke into a smile. "Perhaps their home was purchased through the sale of forged paintings!"

In time Robin Mitchell was repeating Warren Bradley's privately spoken words of caution to others. At the Waterfront Beautification Association monthly meeting, she announced to a small group who hung on her every word, "Both of the Grants are a little full of themselves, don't you think? These two immigrants from the cutthroat business of Manhattan art galleries should be approached with caution!"

CHAPTER NINE

Some of the storm warnings regarding their deteriorating social standing blew back to Barbara and Grant. Their concern, however, was always tempered by the Siricas' advice not to take seriously the negative sentiments of small town folks with too much time on their hands.

As much as Grant enjoyed his work with Sausalito's small but very active arts community, and Barbara continued to frequently put on her laptop's screen photos taken from their home's patio, the town's insular nature began to wear on both of them.

She thoroughly enjoyed working with Anna Moss. The aging gallery owner still moved with boundless energy. Her passion reinvigorated all Barbara loved and missed about the world of art sales.

Regularly, Anna would come to her with a digital portfolio of a new artist and ask her opinion. "Is he too daring for us?" was invariably Anna's first question. "I think of our artists as a blend of different styles—all unique, of course, but they work well together; otherwise you'll never be able to cultivate a collector to move from one artist to another."

Anna's experience came through in everything she said and did.

What Barbara enjoyed most was Anna's urging her to share her opinion. "I want to know what you think, Mrs. Randolph. I have not met anyone more in tune with collectors than you."

Barbara equally enjoyed getting to know Anna's forty-six-year-old son, James. She felt an attraction to him since the first day they met at the gallery.

James, she soon learned, had divorced two years earlier. As he told her, "I doubt that I'll ever find my true soulmate."

Barbara, ever the optimist, insisted, "None of us know what tomorrow might bring. The perfect woman for you might come walking through the gallery's front door next week, and all your pessimism will vanish as if it never existed."

"What if that woman already walked in, and she's you?" James asked in his half-teasing, half-serious fashion.

James didn't have the raw physical appeal of Grant, but he had a level of sensitivity that her husband had in short supply. James' eyes were a remarkable blend of blue and green. His face was open and kind. And while it would have been impossible for her to explain, a small thrill went through her whenever he laughed and gently patted her hand.

Watching Barbara and her son together, Anna told her privately one quiet afternoon, "Be careful my dear. When James wants, he can be very charming. He's much more like his father than I had ever thought possible."

Barbara laughed. "James is wonderful, but I assure you, my Grant is man enough for me."

Still, as the commuter bus taking her home that evening

crawled along the busy approach to the Golden Gate Bridge, Barbara found herself staring out the window and wondering what James would be like to hold in her arms. Would his kisses be tender? Would his lovemaking be a little less fierce, and hopefully more patient, than Grant's?

She had to admit a degree of curiosity. But she did not intend to ever follow her curiosity until, at a reception for the budding young geniuses that made up the Gate Six Artists' Cooperative, she met Grant's latest prodigy, Kitty.

Twice during the evening event, she caught a glimpse of them sharing a joke. At one point, when Grant wandered off to another artist's studio, Barbara made it a point to strike up a conversation with Kitty Collins.

"We have two artists at the Moss Gallery in San Francisco where I work, who use a similar blend of colors and materials," Barbara said, hoping to appear relaxed when she wasn't. "You should come into the city one day, and we can have lunch."

Kitty seemed disinterested and distracted. "I should ask Grant if he'd like to go into the city with me. All three of us could have lunch together."

Everything Barbara disliked about Kitty doubled with that one comment.

It didn't help that she was ten or more years Barbara's junior, with high cheekbones, ash tinted blond hair, exotic brown eyes, and breasts that were all but falling out of her snug white cotton dress.

Call it a woman's intuition or just put it down to the glances she saw them exchange, but for the first time in many years, Barbara wondered if Grant had fallen victim to his once-substantial sexual appetites.

Before coming to Sausalito, Grant had ended the distractions that frequently arose in their marriage whenever he found himself interested in another woman. Barbara was never sure if it was merely lustful curiosity, a playful nature, or a flirtation with more serious implications. After all, when she met Grant, he was involved with that alluring Jamaican woman.

Barbara now wondered if his pursuit of the perfect physique had done more than renew Grant's interest in their shared lovemaking. Perhaps it had also sparked an appetite for new sexual conquests.

There was a part of Barbara that desperately wanted to share her suspicions with Grant, but she couldn't bring herself to do that, fearing she would appear both needy and insecure.

When she arrived home after a busy Saturday at the Moss Gallery, she detected a scent and a presence in her home she'd never noticed before. As she wandered from room to room, she convinced herself that the scent was identical to the perfume worn by Kitty Collins.

It was going on eight. Grant was not home, and there was no note and no cell phone message. Between the imagined scent and the disturbing image of Kitty's overflowing breasts on the night of the artists' reception, Barbara convinced herself that Grant was having an affair.

A burning anger rose from deep inside her. She decided to extinguish that anger with a succession of ice-chilled margaritas. Barbara fell asleep on the couch, wondering if Grant and his pet had made love there as well.

Mistakenly, Grant thought this Saturday was Barbara's evening reception at the Moss Gallery for the opening of a new exhibit, which was actually scheduled for the following Saturday. So, when Ray mentioned that Debbie was spending the night up in Healdsburg with a girlfriend visiting from Chicago and suggested that they have a beer at his place after their workout, Grant thought for a moment, and then said, "Why not?"

Ray threw a couple of steaks on the grill while the two men shared a couple of beers. It was a mild night, so they sat outside, swapping stories about some of the interesting characters that they had met at Golds. There was the guy who did deadlifts while releasing a grunt that could be heard across the entire gym. Another man who, both Ray and Grant agreed, must have dropped a weight on his head at some point was equally bizarre. He stopped them both in the locker room one afternoon and asked if they were a gay couple.

Ray, not at all pleased by the question, replied, "Why the hell would you ask that?"

The fellow looked down at the floor for a moment, trying to recall what gave him that idea, then looked up and said, "I don't know. I guess it's because I always see you both together."

"We share a ride, and we spot for each other when doing bench presses," Ray said with obvious annoyance as he loudly shut his locker's door.

Grant, who was lacing up his shoes, avoided eye contact with either of them. Still, he chuckled to himself. He thought it made no sense for Ray to get irritated with a guy who struggled to utter a single coherent thought.

By the time the steaks and a six pack of beer had been finished, and Ray had pulled out some very special Tequila Clase Azul for both of them to sample, and then taste again, Grant rose with some difficulty and announced: "Barbara should be back from her gallery reception by now."

"Want me to drive you home?" Ray asked.

Grant shook his head. "It's probably better if I walked. We don't want Sausalito's finest making you their big get of the night."

Ray nodded. "Yeah, I guess you're right. Besides, this isn't New York or Chicago. The scariest thing you'll run into in Sausalito late at night is a family of raccoons raiding a trash can."

* * *It was close to midnight when Barbara awoke and called out to Grant.

When there was no answer, she mumbled aloud, "He's still not home! Where the hell is that louse?"

She walked over to the kitchen counter where she had placed her cell phone earlier and started stabbing her fingers against the phone's cold glass touchscreen. Bringing up her "favorite contacts," she angrily pressed, "GRANT."

But her husband, who had left his phone on silent from the time he had entered the gym and then forgot to reset it during his time with Ray, was blissfully unaware of Barbara's several attempts to reach him.

A few minutes later, when he walked through the door in a relaxed but inebriated state, a ripened grapefruit flew past his head, hitting the back of the front door with a dull thud.

Barbara shouted, "Where have you been, you bastard?"

Grant's fog-shrouded mind immediately sensed trouble. He

knew he was under attack, but he was bewildered as to the cause.

"Out late with your little whore girlfriend?"

"WHAT? WHO?"

"You heard me, you lying, cheating dirt bag!"

"What the hell are you talking about?"

Enraged, Barbara came rushing toward him. She was carrying an oversized hardcover coffee table book—a three-hundred-page retrospective on the work of Salvador Dali.

Grant's adrenaline surged. Wildly, he swung his right arm forward to block the book from striking the side of his head. He missed the book, but his powerful forearm cracked across Barbara's lower left cheek and jaw, and sent her reeling backward and crashing to the floor.

Barbara let loose with a bloodcurdling scream as she went down.

The commotion woke their neighbors, the Andersons. Concerned, they called the Sausalito police department. It was after midnight. The town was as peaceful as an undiscovered tomb—a quiet that was shattered needlessly by two patrol cars, blue lights flashing, racing up Bulkley Avenue.

The patrol officers, Hansen and Harding, knocked on the Randolphs' front door less than three minutes after they were summoned.

Grant, who had run to Barbara's side to make a tearful apology, rushed to the door when he heard a deep booming voice say, "Sausalito police! Open up!"

Reeking of beer, sweat, and tequila, Grant pulled open the door. Immediately, he muttered, "Everything is okay, officers."

"Sir, is that your wife on the floor?" Harding asked, "We'll have to check on her condition."

He didn't wait for Grant's response. Instead, he strode to Barbara's side. She was still laying flat on the floor. Looking up in a daze at the eager young faces of the two officers she heard them say, "Ma'am, are you alright? Do you need medical assistance?"

On top of suffering from a surprisingly powerful hit, she had struck the back of her head when she hit the bare tiled floor. Barbara, whose head was ringing, responded groggily to the officers' questions, none of which they could comprehend.

Hansen called the fire department to send up the EMT crew.

Meanwhile, Harding took out his handcuffs. Before Grant fully understood what was happening, he had been restrained and was being escorted out the front door.

The officers drove him up to the county jail for processing on a charge of assault and battery.

A stretcher was brought in, and in less than a clear voice, Barbara said she thought it was unnecessary to take her to the county hospital, Marin General. But the EMT officers insisted, explaining that it was a precaution whenever someone had suffered a blow to the back of the head.

Oscar and Clarice Anderson, both in their early-eighties, watched in horror from their upstairs bedroom window as Grant Randolph was taken out in handcuffs, followed a short time later by his wife being taken on a gurney into the back of a Sausalito Fire Department medical transport vehicle.

"Oh, my God!" Clarice exclaimed. "They seemed like such a nice quiet couple!"

Oscar held his arm around his wife's shoulders. "Looks can be deceiving, my dear."

They turned out their lights and returned to bed.

CHAPTER TEN

After Chris Harding and Steve Hansen's retelling of the midnight domestic violence call to the Randolph home, and after Alma insisted that Bradley use his "Heard About Town" column to call for Grant Randolph's removal from the arts commission, Warren had few remaining options. He needed to act as the swift hand of public justice or risk losing most of his column's biggest fans.

He knew the why but was puzzled by the how. Then a thought occurred to him: Who might have overheard the Randolphs' battle and its aftermath?

Late Monday he called Bea, a living Who's Who of Sausalito's small army of community volunteers. He asked her who lived on Bulkley Avenue next door to, or nearby, the Randolphs. Once he heard about Clarice and Oscar Anderson, he asked Bea if they were active on any of the town's volunteer committees. Bea thought for a moment and recalled them both helping the library foundation prepare for their annual community book sale.

Thirty minutes later, Warren was busy mixing up his irresistible cherry-fudge brownies.

Oscar and Clarice knew Warren through his volunteer efforts but had never read his weekly column. Instead, when *The Standard* hit their mailbox every Wednesday, they gave the front page a quick glance and then dropped it into the recycling bin.

The Andersons were a quiet couple who had lived in Sausalito for over forty years. They'd raised two children and were strict adherents to the rule of minding your own business.

Early on Tuesday, they were surprised to find Warren on their doorstep with a platter of cherry-fudge brownies.

"Warren, this is so nice of you!" Clarice declared as she welcomed him into her home. "Why the unexpected visit?"

"Bea and I were talking about how helpful the two of you were in organizing those stacks of library books that had been removed from circulation and placed in the community book sale. I just thought it would be nice if I made you a batch of these yummy treats."

Oscar and Clarice said in unison, "You must stay and have a cup of tea or coffee with us."

Warren fussed over accepting their invitation, pretending he didn't want to interrupt their day, but it was precisely what he had hoped would happen. He followed the couple into their cluttered and dated living room and said a silent prayer that the Andersons were not in bed with their hearing aids turned off when the police came to Barbara Randolph's rescue.

Over tea, they tasted Warren's creation and agreed that the brownies were delicious. Clarice asked, "Warren, would you be kind enough to share the recipe? These are just divine!"

Warren hesitated for a moment, as though he was sharing something of great value. "They're an old family recipe...but alright, my dear. I'll send you an email with the ingredients and directions. But, please, keep it between us."

In truth, the recipe came out of a stack of old *Bon Appétit* magazines housed in the storage room of the Sausalito Library.

Warren probed with a line he had dreamt up while standing over his stove, whipping up the chocolate sauce topping for his cherry-fudge brownies. "One thing I love about this upper part of Bulkley is how quiet it is up here."

Oscar frowned. "Well, it's not quiet all the time."

"Why, whatever do you mean by that?" Warren asked innocently.

Oscar and Clarice looked at each other wondering who would speak first. Clarice decided to enter the void. "Sunday morning—a little past midnight, if you can believe that—we had quite a bit of excitement up here! Oscar was asleep, and I was sitting up trying to finish an old Agatha Christie *Miss Marple* mystery when I heard what sounded like shouting coming from next door."

"Oh, my!" Warren exclaimed. "What was that all about?"

"The Randolphs were having one heck of a fight, that's what," Oscar declared. "We got up and went to the window to see what was going on."

"When I heard what I felt certain was Barbara Randolph's scream, I immediately dialed 911," Clarisse added. "Seeing Grant Randolph in handcuffs, Barbara Randolph being wheeled out on a stretcher, it was all so shocking and so sad. They seemed like the nicest couple."

Warren shook his head sadly.

After further chitchat and mutually concluding that "the Randolphs should get counseling, so nothing like this ever happens again," Warren left.

Walking quickly back to his car, Warren had to fight an impulse to jump for joy just in case the Andersons were peering out from behind their living room curtains.

Just hours before his weekly deadline, Bradley scrapped the part of his "Heard About Town" column on the ongoing dispute over permitting local restaurants the option of providing sidewalk dining, and substituted a new lead that practically wrote itself. It was, of course, the Randolph story:

The peace and tranquility of Bulkley Avenue, home to many of Sausalito's best families, was suddenly shattered after midnight Sunday morning by a violent argument between Grant and Barbara Randolph, as reported by their neighbors Clarice and Oscar Anderson.

Sausalito Police confirmed that the violent dispute led to Mr. Randolph's arrest and Mrs. Randolph being rushed to Marin General Hospital over concern that she had suffered possibly life-threatening injuries during their altercation.

Ethel Landau, a longtime member and former chair of the Sausalito Fine Arts Commission, which Mr. Randolph was recently made the chairman of, called the incident "shocking and greatly disappointing." Adding, "In light of these developments, it's perhaps time we reconsider Mr. Randolph's participation with the commission."

Neither Grant nor Barbara Randolph, who recently relocated to Sausalito from the often-violent streets of New York City, were avail-

able at press time for comment. Undoubtedly, we'll have more on this story in the coming weeks.

🌸

This time, Rob read Warren's column before it went on press.

Once again, he was not pleased. Still, Rob knew that this kind of celebrity magazine salaciousness was catnip for many readers. Warren's column, after all, was only read by most for its occasional items of local gossip.

Nevertheless, Rob called Warren. "I assume you've covered your back on this story and double-checked your facts?"

"Absolutely, Rob," Warren said with great confidence. "I got the bare bone facts on Monday from two police officers who responded to the 911 call. I then visited the Randolphs' neighbors, the Andersons, on Tuesday. They watched the entire thing from their bedroom window. They witnessed Grant Randolph being taken out in handcuffs, and Barbara Randolph wheeled out on a stretcher and placed in an ambulance."

"I don't think Grant Randolph will be coming to your next birthday party, but I assume you're okay with that," Rob retorted.

"That's fine with me. I'd never invite the brute anyway."

After Warren had hung up the phone, he sat back in his favorite chair.

He had kept his promise to Chief Petersen not to make his department the only source of information regarding the Randolph incident. Of course, there was now an additional public record of the arrest. And if Barbara pressed charges, any subsequent trial would be in the court's public records as well.

But, as a local columnist, the essential ingredient was the commotion disturbing the peaceful night of the Randolphs' elderly neighbors. The Andersons, having awakened after midnight and horrified to see what was happening next door, were the simple touch of community that made the entire story work perfectly.

Best of all, even with a tight deadline, Warren accomplished all his goals in what, for him, was record time.

Warren brewed a cup of tea and sat down to enjoy his reward: a just-baked fruit crisp, which had the perfect blend of sweet and sour tastes.

CHAPTER ELEVEN

This week's "Heard About Town" column was suddenly the talk of the town. Alma and the Ladies of Liberty had nothing but praise for what she heralded as "Warren's courageous, insightful, and powerful reporting."

Warren could hardly contain his joy. This was undoubtedly a perfect week. He had inflicted real social damage to the Randolphs, and he had endeared himself to those he often referred to as, "All the right people."

But his delight was mixed with some caution. He knew that for a time it would be ill-advised for him to drive or walk down Bulkley Avenue, attend a meeting of the Sausalito Fine Arts Commission, or an open house at the Gate Six Artists' Cooperative—all proof that, as he told himself repeatedly, good investigative journalism often comes at the price of one's personal safety.

"Are you at all concerned that you have most likely enraged a very dangerous man?" Bea asked Warren breathlessly.

"Reporting the facts is part of any journalist's job; you have to take certain risks if you're ever going to be true to your mission," Warren proclaimed as he pouted his lips forward and stood with an air of resolve worthy of a general.

Bea, admiring his determination, felt deeply moved to be in the presence of such a fearless individual.

Three days before Warren's column rocked Sausalito, the Randolphs sat down together for the first time. It occurred before noon on Sunday, two hours after Ray suggested to Barbara that he go up to the jail to bring Grant back home.

Debbie, having returned from her Saturday overnight trip to Sonoma County, went directly to check on her friend Barbara. She winced when Barbara opened her front door. The mid-morning light caught the discoloration and swelling along her friend's jawline.

Debbie put out her arms, and for a while, the two women hugged and held each other in silence.

"What happened?" Debbie asked soft, but urgent tone.

"It was so fast, it seems like a blur now. To be honest, it doesn't make a lot of sense!" Barbara admitted.

She recalled expecting to find Grant at home Saturday night when she returned from the city. He wasn't. Far worse, she suspected he had been in their home earlier with another woman, undoubtedly when she was working in the city. Barbara then told Debbie about Kitty Collins and her suspicions regarding Grant's attraction to her.

It occurred to Debbie to say that Grant would never do

such a thing, but she held back, deciding it would be wiser to quietly listen.

Barbara explained that she had made herself a margarita, followed by a second and a third. Afterward, she drifted off on the couch, waking near midnight to find Grant still not home. "By that point, I was very angry and very disappointed."

Debbie held her hand and continued to listen.

"I looked at the clock, and then I looked at the front door. The longer I sat there, the angrier I got," Barbara added. "When Grant came home, I just flew into a rage! It wasn't what I thought I would do, but all this anger just came out. I went at him or threw something at him. I don't remember exactly what. Then, bang! I'm on the floor. I must have blacked out for a bit because the next thing I know, this Sausalito cop is standing over me."

Debbie squeezed Barbara's hand as her eyes welled up again. In a soft voice, Barbara continued. "Then there were more of these guys standing around me. They placed me on a stretcher. I wanted to ask where the hell they were taking me, but my throat just seemed to swell shut, and it swallowed my voice. Before that, I looked over and saw Grant with his arms behind his back and a police officer walking him out the front door! I thought this must be a nightmare." She wiped tears away. "It was all so unreal. Nothing like this has ever happened to Grant or me. Never!"

"I know nothing about Saturday night other than what I heard from Ray," Debbie admitted. "But I can tell you this. Grant and Ray went to the gym in the late afternoon, and then they went back to our house, cooked out, and both had, as Ray told me, way too much to drink."

"Why didn't Grant come home after the gym?"

"I asked Ray that. He said Grant told him you were staying late at the gallery for an open house."

"That's next Saturday night. I was home before seven and wondering why he wasn't here. I called his cell, three times at least. He never picked up," Barbara explained, relieved that at least some of what happened Saturday night was beginning to make sense.

Ray picked up Grant after a bondsman posted his bail.

On the twelve-mile drive back from San Rafael to Sausalito, Ray could not resist the overwhelming temptation to ask, "What the hell happened? If I realized you were going to go home last night and coldcock your wife, I would have told you to stay in one of our guest rooms and sleep it off!"

Grant, who had spent a sleepless night thinking about Barbara, wondered how, in a matter of minutes, he'd gone from a respected name in the art world to sitting in a jail cell charged with assaulting his wife.

"I spent the night trying to figure out what happened. I know we both got hammered. I know I came home, and Barbara came at me like I was an ax murderer who just broke into the house, but the rest of it doesn't add up!"

Ray winced. "It sounds like a big mess to me. Debbie is over at your place right now. Maybe together we can figure out what the hell happened."

"I know one thing. As I walked through the door, my head was buzzing. I heard Barbara scream out something; I looked up and saw her coming at me with one of those oversized art books we have all around the house. I swung my arm out in the dumbest move of my life to avoid getting whacked over the head and caught her right on the jaw. She screamed, went down, and everything else after that happened pretty fast."

"Okay, pal, I just have to ask: Has anything like this ever happened before?"

"No, absolutely not! I would never intentionally injure my wife."

When Ray walked through the door of the Randolph home, both he and Debbie froze for a moment.

Grant stood by the doorway and looked at Barbara.

Barbara silently stared at Grant.

The silence for a few moments was deafening. Then, Barbara stood, and Grant rushed toward her.

They hugged and cried. Debbie dabbed away tears from the corners of her eyes.

Ray put his arm around Debbie's shoulders and whispered, "I think that's our cue to get the hell out of here."

Debbie nodded. As they turned to leave, she looked back and saw her two closest friends holding each other, completely unaware of the presence of anyone else in the room.

That afternoon, Grant and Barbara unraveled the mystery of what had happened fourteen hours earlier.

It took Barbara time before she could raise the issue of Kitty. Grant acknowledged that there was sexual tension between the two of them and that Kitty, in her free-spirited way, had made it clear that she was open to both of them following their desires wherever they led.

Having explained that, Grant cuddled in beside Barbara on the couch and said, "Together, you and I have spent a lot of time around artists; we know they can be pretty casual about intimacy. I'd be lying if I told you that I don't find Kitty attractive and tempting, I think a lot of guys would. But, it's like this…"

While Grant gathered his thoughts, Barbara kissed him softly on the cheek. Finally, he began: "If you love someone, you have to be invested deeply in your relationship. Temptation comes along one or more times, but if you give into that desire, it's like cutting a hole in the bottom of your pocket. Everything you are together is because of what you have shared in the past and are hoping to share in the future. If you're not careful, all of that, just like gold coins, can fall out the bottom of your pocket and be lost. Perhaps, forever. That's not a smart thing to do."

Barbara nodded, "Is that your way of saying you don't want to lose what we've built together?"

"Absolutely! With all my heart."

They spent the rest of Sunday afternoon in bed, naked, wrapped tightly around each other.

Moving his head up from where his lips caressed her neck,

reaching for her mouth, Grant grazed her bruised jaw and saw Barbara wince. He gently kissed her and told her again how deeply sorry he was.

"Perhaps I should lay off the strength training."

"Are you kidding? I love your arms, and I love your shoulders! Just don't take a swing in my direction and I'll be happy. You don't know it, but you can pack one helluva wallop."

"It's a deal. And you promise not to crown me with any oversized coffee table art books because I've done something stupid."

They kissed and laughed. Exhausted from two days and one very long night with little if any rest, they both fell into a deep sleep.

For the next few days, the Randolphs happily hid from the rest of the world.

On Wednesday, with home delivery of *The Standard*, the darker side of life in a town where everyone knows your name, found them once again.

CHAPTER TWELVE

Ray was the first to notice the lead in Bradley's "Heard About Town" column.

He called out, "Oh my God! Debbie, you've got to get in here!"

As Debbie read, all the color went out of her face. She became so angry at what Warren had written that she started to shake.

"That malicious little man! This is just disgraceful! Raymond, what are you going to do about this?"

"What do you mean, what am *I* going to do?"

"I don't know what I mean," she retorted. "When we were telling Grant and Barbara what a beautiful and peaceful place Sausalito is, we never dreamed of anything like this."

"What I'd like to do," Ray said, "is pick up that nasty little troll by the scruff of his neck and slap him senseless."

"But what you'd like to do, and what you can do, Ray, are two different things."

They both sat silently for a moment, staring out at a picture book view of the bay.

"Should we call Barbara and Grant?" Debbie asked.

"I've never heard them say a word about looking at *The Standard*, although I guess Grant checks it for coverage of the arts commission if nothing else."

They toyed with the thought that perhaps their friends would not see the piece, but decided that was wishful thinking. One of his fellow commission members was sure to ask Grant about what happened.

"We have to let them know what this little weasel Bradley put in the paper," Ray said, regretting there was no other logical thing to do. "Deb, call them and see if they're home; tell them we have something we need to share with them."

The Siricas arrived at the Grants to find them blissfully enjoying their day. Barbara made client calls that morning from home. She and Grant decided to spend the afternoon working together on the small garden that hugged their side patio.

Debbie and Ray knew that they would be ruining what appeared to be a peaceful moment, but they resolved it was better for the two of them to hear this news from friends.

Barbara insisted that they sit down at the patio table and she would bring out something to drink. Her guests sat down but waved off the beverages.

The bruising along Barbara's left jawline was already much improved but remained visible. Grant, still uncomfortable over the embarrassment of what the two of them now called "The mother of all misunderstandings," pulled off the gardening gloves he had been weeding with and sat down as well.

Debbie smiled and pushed Ray's knee under the table, as if to say: Please, go first!

Ray pulled the new issue of *The Standard* from his back pocket. He laid the paper on the table and opened it to Bradley's column.

"That spat you two had was picked up in the local gossip column—"

The words were hardly out of Ray's mouth when Grant grabbed the paper and started to read the first few paragraphs of Warren's column.

With his voice rising, and with Barbara's face reddening, Grant read, "Sausalito Police confirmed that the violent dispute led to Mr. Randolph's arrest and Mrs. Randolph being rushed to Marin General Hospital over concern that she had suffered possibly life-threatening injuries during their altercation."

Grant was annoyed by Ethel Landau's suggestion, quoted in the following paragraph, that it might be time for the commission to "reconsider Mr. Randolph's participation."

"I'll quit before they ever have the chance to ask me to step aside!" Grant said, as his face reddened in anger.

But what most angered both Grant and Barbara was Warren's claim that at press time, neither of the Randolphs were available for comment.

"That's complete bullshit!" Grant said as he slammed the paper down on the table.

Barbara grabbed it off the table and reread the story in silence. When she had finished, in a soft voice she said, "This is awful, just awful!"

After a few moments of silence, Ray, the only one of the three of them not intimidated by Grant's anger, said, "I don't like that little gnome any more than you do, Grant, but we all know what he wrote isn't a total fabrication."

"I don't mean what he said about the fight. That was mostly true—although I think he deliberately over-dramatized Barbara's condition. What ticks me off is this bullshit about neither of us being available for comment at press time," Grant explained.

"In other words," Ray said, "you think the SOB was avoiding you because he didn't want your comments, knowing you'd at least try to explain what happened."

"Exactly! He wanted to put our situation in the worst light possible, right down to his wisecrack, making it sound as if we just arrived here off the set of *Gangs of New York*."

"I do not doubt that. With my having the last name of Sirica, Bradley would gladly imply that I'm a retired Chicago mobster! In truth, he's lucky my dad was in the pajama game, and not in the Cosa Nostra. Otherwise, Warren would be on his way right now to the bottom of Richardson Bay in cement pajamas."

With that, the four of them shared a much-needed laugh. Afterward, each imagined how much better a place their community would be if Warren Bradley was entombed in cement and deposited into the quiet waters between Sausalito and Tiburon.

Barbara tried to take this latest social setback in stride. "Between the hatchet job Bradley did on me for turning down the league's invitation, and now our knock-down, drag-out fight, maybe I should get fitted for a burqa for when Debbie and I take one of our walks through town."

Barbara's suggestion broke the tension, to Ray and Debbie's relief.

At that moment, the four close friends looked up as they heard the gate on the white picket fence open and shut. Oscar and Clarice Anderson were walking toward them. Clarice was dabbing her eyes with a handkerchief. After exchanging greetings and an introduction to Ray and Debbie, Oscar said, "Clarice and I just read what that awful man, Bradley, wrote about the two of you. We never read *The Standard*, and we didn't even know about his column."

"How'd you find out?" Ray asked.

"A friend called us to tell us that our names were in the paper!" Clarice explained. "So, we fished the paper out of the recycling bin. That's what happens every week—it comes in the mail, we look at the front page to see if there's any news that concerns us—street repairs, bond measures and such— then we put it in recycling."

"Do you even know Warren Bradley?" Grant asked.

"Oh, sure. We're on the library volunteer committee with him," Oscar said.

"When he showed up at our house with a plate of brownies we, of course, invited him in," Clarice explained. "We were both surprised to see him. He's never done anything like that before."

"When we saw his column today, we realized why he had been so nice," Oscar added with a scowl.

"I'm so sorry about all this," Clarice sobbed. "I'm even sorry that we called the police! But when we heard Barbara scream, we didn't know what was happening."

Barbara, tearing up, stood up and embraced Clarice. "Don't cry, dear. This all started over a stupid misunderstanding; both of us had way too much to drink, and everything from that point on got out of control."

Grant's face reddened with feelings of both anger and embarrassment.

After hugs were exchanged, the Andersons left. Clarice was still dabbing away tears as they sauntered back toward the white picket fence.

As Ray and Debbie got up to leave, Grant declared, "If I ever see Bradley again at a meeting of the arts commission, I'm going to wring that wicked little man's neck."

"Don't do anything to make things worse, pal," Ray warned him. "This will all die down in a week or two. Until then, if you should run into Bradley, do yourself a favor and keep your hands in your pockets."

Every Saturday evening in spring, The Sausalito Opera Society, SOS, holds an outdoor performance at Gabrielson Park, which is within steps of the ferry landing and the Sausalito Yacht Club.

The mild evening air and that evening's performance, featuring selections from Verdi's *La Traviata,* brought out what was likely the event's biggest opening night crowd ever.

Almost all the town's residents—especially those who served on various governmental and social committees—were in attendance: the five members of the city council, members of the city's numerous commissions: planning, design review, historical, parks and recreation, and fine arts.

Also present were most of the Sausalito Women's League

members, several of whom served on the committee that arranged refreshments for the night.

Most notably Alma, and her Ladies of Liberty, who sat at one of the several tables reserved for distinguished guests and local officials.

Grant decided not to sit at the table reserved for the arts commission, choosing instead to join Barbara, Ray, and Debbie on a blanket spread on the park's thick green grass. At first, Barbara resisted the suggestion of attending. It had only been three days since Warren's column had appeared, and Barbara dreaded the curious stares that most certainly would come at them from all directions.

"I'm not sure I'm ready to be seen in public. I'm still waiting for that burqa I ordered to arrive," Barbara explained to Grant, only half-jokingly.

Debbie had also been ambivalent about attending the event, but like Grant, Ray had countered, "People like Warren Bradley are not going to spoil this, or any night in Sausalito, for us."

Now that they were there and the evening air was so pleasant, and the wine and covered dishes they had brought were so delicious, the four friends relaxed. Barbara noticed a few raised eyebrows, mostly coming from Robin Mitchell and others seated at the Ladies of Liberty table. There were a few whispers into cupped ears and nods aimed in their direction, but Barbara disciplined herself to focus on the music and the setting, pushing every other thought aside.

During intermission, the four friends noticed Warren buzzing from table to table like a busy bee pollinating half-truths, smiling, laughing, and greeting those he considered his social set. With each of Warren's extended chuckles, Barbara suspected that she and her husband were the targets of most, if not all, of his quips. Again, she pushed aside her irritation and willed herself to ignore a nagging sense of humiliation.

It wasn't until later, after the final aria of the evening when everyone was packing up their blankets and picnic baskets, that Grant walked over and tapped Warren Bradley on the shoulder. If Barbara, Ray, or Debbie knew what Grant was about to do, they would have made every effort to stop him.

Perhaps his original intent was, as he explained later, to say hello to a few of his fellow arts commission members. But when he passed so close to Warren, he could feel his anger rising like a force of nature desperately seeking release. Grant could not hold back.

Warren's look of feigned innocence and barely disguised delight added to Grant's fury. The social gadfly reasoned he was safe while surrounded by so many of his fellow citizens and devoted admirers. Grant's right hand formed into a fist. How easy it would be to permanently wipe that smirk off Bradley's face. But inside, he could hear that controlling half of his mind shouting, *No, you cannot, must not, do that!*

Instead, Grant settled for dressing down his nemesis: "That was a cheap shot you took at me in your column!"

Sausalito's core group of busybodies scattered around the two of them, hoping to appear as if they were looking away while desperately trying to hear every word and witness every action.

"Now, Grant, calm down!" In truth, Warren was thrilled that Grant had risen to his bait. All night long he'd whispered this mantra to any ear open to hearing it: "Grant Randolph is a dangerous, reckless hothead, who should take his ill manners and questionable breeding back to New York City."

"Don't tell me to calm down," Grant growled. "You knew what you were doing when you wrote that bullshit about my not being available for comment. You didn't want to hear what I had to say because the truth would have damaged your snide, slanted little story."

At this point, Grant's voice was loud enough for fans of both opera and local drama to hear. Given an audience, Warren said in a raised voice, "Would someone please tell a police officer that I'm feeling threatened by this man?"

Ray walked over and took Grant's arm. Instinctively, Grant jerked it away.

Everyone held their collective breaths just as Chris Harding stepped in. "What seems to be the problem, Mr. Bradley?"

Warren, much relieved to have the tall, muscular, young police officer at his side, used the opportunity to pour a little salt into Grant's profoundly wounded reputation. "Officer, Mr. Randolph seems to be agitated about my column in *The Standard* this week. I'm beginning to fear for my safety!"

If looks could kill, Grant's anger would have dispatched Warren to a better—or perhaps a far worse place, at that very moment.

Nonchalantly, Harding declared, "Okay, well if we're done here, let's just pack up and move along."

Anxious to get his friend away from Bradley as soon as possible, Ray put his arm around Grant. "Come on, let's get out of here. This is enough excitement for one night."

For a few moments longer, Grant stood his ground. Finally, he turned his back on Warren and walked away, aware that the muscles in his arms were twitching and his fists clenching.

As Grant moved along, he scanned the people around the small park, all of whom were staring back at him. But it was

Barbara and Debbie's horrified expressions that validated what he already knew: he'd taken a bad situation and made it worse.

Grant was still steaming the next day when he and Ray made their daily pilgrimage to Gold's Gym. Again, he thanked Ray for taking hold of him. "I so wanted to wipe the smirk off that idiot's face. Thanks for coming over and saving me."

"Nothing you wouldn't have done for me. Listen, if you want to step on this knucklehead's throat and you've got a few bucks lying around, talk to a lawyer. Find out if you can sue him and the newspaper that prints his column."

It was an idea that Grant, in all his anger, hadn't seriously considered.

Later that night, he went online to Martindale.com and checked the reviews of several local attorneys. Finally, he chose one to call to arrange an appointment. He decided to keep mum about it to Barbara, though, because he wanted to present her with the possibility of taking a civil approach to beating that irksome, mean-spirited man.

"But look what this guy did to my wife and me!" Grant retorted. He pushed the article under the nose of attorney, Bob Ivan.

Bob's credentials were impeccable. He was revered at the county courthouse for being wise, considerate—and best of all, someone you never wanted to go up against in a courtroom.

With bright blue eyes that did not look possible for a man in his mid-seventies, Ivan had the quiet demeanor of a country lawyer, which belied the savvy of a top-flight attorney with an unmatched string of courtroom victories.

"Don't get me wrong, Grant," Ivan explained patiently. "If I were you, I'd want to wring the SOB's neck as well. But the courts are loath to sit in judgment of a free press."

"Why should this character get a free ride because he writes for a newspaper?"

"Simple. Because local judges, who are elected officials, are not anxious to get into cases in which press rights are challenged in the absence of strong facts. And from what you told me, nothing he wrote in his column was factually inaccurate. I do not doubt that he put the story in the worst light possible, but in no way does this rise to the legal definition of libel."

"But he lied when he wrote that we were not available for comment!"

"I'm sure you're right about that as well. The problem is that's all but impossible to prove." With his right hand, Ivan brushed away a cowlick of chalk-white hair from his forehead. "I have absolutely no doubt that this Bradley fellow is a loathsome character; that he cherry-picked facts and is not playing fair. A judge might think that as well. Still, no judge is going to hold him to account as to whether or not he dialed the right number when calling you for a comment."

As reluctant as Grant was to admit it, he knew Bob was right.

The next day at the gym he shared with Ray the story of his meeting with Bob Ivan.

"Sounds like a stand-up guy," Ray conceded.

Grant nodded. "I got that impression, too. I just wished there was something he could do about Bradley!"

Ray snorted. "This is why people take matters into their own hands. In the neighborhood I grew up in, Warren Bradley would have been taken for a ride a long time ago. And I'll promise you this—no one would have missed him."

CHAPTER THIRTEEN

Warren was experiencing a season of good fortune. First, there was the domestic upheaval at the Randolphs, followed by Grant's Saturday evening confrontation at the conclusion of Sausalito's Night at the Opera. That the incident was witnessed by all the people Warren attempted to please was an unanticipated bonus.

It was in this state of bliss that Warren sat down Monday morning to write his next piece, which began with the headline: "New Concerns Surface Regarding Arts Commission Chair Grant Randolph."

After setting the scene—reporting on every detail of the event from the arias performed to what Alma Samuels, Robin Mitchell, Ethel Landau and Bea Snyder wore—Warren arrived at his fourth paragraph and delivered his intended message:

Suddenly, the magic of this perfect evening was shattered when Mr. Grant Randolph accosted this columnist over a story shared in last week's column, detailing an act of domestic violence.

Randolph, who chairs the city's prestigious fine arts commission,

*was booked and spent the night in San Rafael at the county's prison
facility one week before the opera event. As Randolph was taken
away in handcuffs, Mrs. Barbara Randolph was rushed to Marin
County Hospital, where she was treated and released after having
been assaulted by her husband.*

*It's easy to understand why Randolph would prefer not to see such
truths displayed in print, but a peaceful community is built on a
foundation of civil behavior.*

*Since this latest incident, new concerns are being raised among
Sausalito's vibrant corps of citizen volunteers. "Do we have a right to
expect community leaders to be held to a higher standard of behavior?" Alma Samuels asked after witnessing Grant Randolph's latest
fit of anger.*

*"It's time our arts commission take a serious look at the indi-
vidual they have chosen to lead their group," Ms. Samuels concluded
moments after Sausalito police officer, Chris Harding, stepped in to
calm the highly agitated Mr. Randolph.*

*We all value the arts, but the peace of our community we value
above all else.*

The following morning, Rob read Warren's latest
salvo, which once again targeted Grant Randolph.
Wincing, he declared, "Holly, get in here and tell me
what you think of Warren's latest."

After reading the piece, Holly shrugged, "If I were this
Randolph guy, I'd want to take a swing at Bradley as well."

Rob was tempted to call Warren and tell him to rework the
piece before press time but then hesitated. If he merely
suggested that Warren tone down his article, he would

undoubtedly go whining to the Ladies of Liberty, claiming that Rob Timmons was preventing him from reporting his entire story. One way or another, Alma's army would try, yet again, to make life difficult for him and his small community newspaper. Previously, they had started a quiet campaign, urging Sausalito merchants to curtail their advertising in the paper because of a series *The Standard* had done on the shortcomings of the Sausalito Police Department. The campaign fizzled because several of the merchants had been victims of overnight robberies.

On that occasion, timing had worked in his favor. This time Rob might not be so lucky.

"You want me to run something in place of his column this week?" Holly asked.

"I think I've got a better idea. Didn't you say you got a couple of letters in yesterday, one from Randolph's wife and one from a friend of his?"

"Yep. Grant's friend, a guy named Ray Sirica wrote a strong letter. So did Randolph's wife, Barbara."

"Okay. Let's slide them alongside Warren's column, put them on top of this week's letters and feature them with a headline, something like 'Speaking up on Behalf of Grant Randolph.'"

"Good thinking, Rob. I'll slot them both into the layout right now," Holly said with a smile as she hurried back to her workstation.

Barbara's letter emphasized that their argument was a "Shakespearean series of tragic misunderstandings," and in no way reflected the actual character of her husband, Grant, who, in reality, "is the most loving and supportive partner any woman could ever hope to have."

Ray's letter was stronger in its approach. "As a longtime friend of Grant and Barbara Randolph, I have known them to be a loving and mutually supportive couple. We all have moments when we're not at our best—times that we would not want a local busybody going through our garbage or deceptively teasing information out of our neighbors. Additionally, Bradley was dishonest in claiming that he had reached out to Barbara and Grant Randolph to get their side of the story. He did no such thing. Neither of the Randolphs' phones showed a missed call or a phone message from Mr. Bradley."

Then, referring to the longstanding, albeit unspoken nickname for Warren that had never before appeared in print, Ray added, "Thankfully, most of us are fortunate enough not to find ourselves in the crosshairs of Warren Bradley, Sausalito's very own, Gossiping Gourmet."

The salvos exchanged in *The Standard* that week did little to quiet the local furor. In fact, it increased attention to the issue.

At local eateries, patrons made the growing dispute between the Randolphs and Warren Bradley the town's number one topic of conversation. Was Bradley merely doing his job by reporting unpleasant facts about a local official, or was he seeking to undermine Grant's position in the community?

To Grant's detractors, Barbara was a "whimpering supplicant." But Ray Sirica's words wounded Warren more deeply. He knew he could have reached out to the Randolphs for comment before going to press with his original story.

Claiming they were "not available at press time" was done with the hope of avoiding any information that might have put their altercation in a far less troubling light.

Ray's portrayal of Warren as "the Gossiping Gourmet," who goes looking through his neighbors' trash to find tidbits to embarrass people, or teases information out of unsuspecting individuals, represented Sirica's attempt to turn Warren the accuser into Warren the accused.

Alma knew one thing for sure: Ray Sirica's letter moved him and his wife into the social freezer. Debbie would, of course, retain her position in the Sausalito League of Women, but she would not be given any role more significant than reindeer herder for their annual follies. Alma worked the phone to make it crystal clear that Debbie Sirica was no longer considered, "One of us!"

CHAPTER FOURTEEN

Having a calendar filled with special events for which he was expected to bring a prepared dish, what Warren enjoyed most was using his cooking skills for those occasions when he entertained at his small hillside cottage.

This particular evening was one he had anticipated for the last two weeks. It presented the opportunity to prepare one of his long-standing favorite dishes: pasta with veal, sausage, and porcini ragu. What a welcome change, Warren thought, from all this commotion regarding Randolph and his unpleasant encounters with both him and his likely mob-connected pal, Ray Sirica!

Soon after Warren arrived in Sausalito, approximately twenty-five years ago, he befriended a childless widow named Lillian Danvers. He cooked for her, did her shopping, and took her to doctor's appointments.

Shortly after she died in her sleep one wet winter's night,

Warren moved into the Danvers home. At the time his doing so raised a few eyebrows among the town's senior set, but to others, it seemed like a reasonable exchange. For over two years he had cared for her, and, if the rumor was true, at one point he had been her "young lover." They had a documented agreement, supposedly memorialized by one of the county's many attorneys, specifying the transfer of the property deed to Warren at the time of her death upon the payment of a single dollar.

Although the home was small compared to the estates of Sausalito's landed gentry, Warren was perfectly happy there. With no plans to start a family, the Danvers cottage met his three greatest expectations: an adequate kitchen, a beautiful bay view, and a home up on the hill, which, to Sausalito society, meant he had arrived.

So engrossed was Warren in the preparation of his favorite sauce that he completely forgot that this evening was also the deadline for his weekly column.

Now that it had finally crossed his mind, he knew there was no hope of his completing the column and also having his meal prepared in time for his special guest. Warren reached for the phone and called Rob, whom he rightly assumed had left his office for the day.

"Hello, Rob," he began, making certain his voicemail conveyed an air of relaxed assurance. "This week's column is nearly complete, I just want to polish it a bit more, but I have plans for the evening. I'll have it for you well before noon tomorrow. It's an important column, and I think you'll like what I've done."

The message was a complete fabrication. In fact, Warren

had no idea what he was going to write, meaning the column's regular length, approximately seven hundred and fifty words, would be more painful to accomplish than usual.

As he lovingly sautéed the veal in a wine sauce until it browned, his mind wandered over a range of possibilities. Alma, Bea, and Robin had told him repeatedly that he needed to keep the heat on Randolph, but the entire episode was placing him in the middle of a dispute that he found increasingly uncomfortable.

While he busied himself slicing onions, carrots, and tomatoes, it occurred to him that perhaps in this week's column he could declare that the moment had arrived for members of the Sausalito Fine Arts Commission to take a stand on the subject of violence against women. Once he settled on his topic, the column began to write itself.

Warren, a master in the nasty business of scheming, knew full well that Sirica was attempting to demean him as a spiteful and frequently dishonest gossipmonger. The only way to extradite himself was to elevate the issue beyond one domestic dispute to a more lofty topic. He intended to tell his readers that the core facts of this story were not of his creation. The police had been summoned! The peace had been disturbed! And when it was over, a citizen of Sausalito, who held a distinguished position in the community, was on his way to the county jail while his wife was being rushed to the hospital with possibly life-threatening injuries! What part of any of this was acceptable behavior?

Warren's resentment for the loathsome Grant Randolph was again rising to a boil. There was no doubt that the muse was present in him at that very moment. At the very least, he had to put his thoughts down in writing. Were he to wait until later that night, his passion might dissipate in the afterglow of a delicious meal, topped off with a bottle or two of that Consorzio Chianti Rufina that he had been saving for a special occasion.

Warren looked at the oversized clock that hung on the wood-paneled kitchen wall. His guest was due to arrive a little after seven, but it was just a few minutes past six. He lifted the lid of each pan to do one more quick check, and then he filled a large pot slightly more than halfway with the water he would use to cook his pasta, putting a low flame below it so it would begin to warm. Warren stepped into his small, cluttered bedroom and sat down at the desk wedged into the room's tiny alcove. He opened an aging, off-brand laptop, and began to state his case for the removal of Randolph from high office:

In the past two weeks, much has been said about the behavior of Sausalito Fine Arts Commission chair, Grant Randolph. His arrest by police, on suspicion of spousal abuse, has no doubt shocked many in our quiet, tight-knit community.

While it now appears clear that Mrs. Randolph has decided not to pursue the matter of assault, it is nonetheless shocking and discomforting that an individual holding an important position in our fair city's cultural life has conducted himself in this manner.

Heard About Town readers know how stridently I have argued for a return to the standards of proper conduct. I do not doubt that the majority of Sausalito's citizens would agree with me that, whatever the final disposition of these charges, Mr. Randolph's conduct falls far short of what any one of us would call civil behavior.

What is perhaps most troubling is how Mr. Randolph's actions reflect poorly on our city's arts commission, an august group that has been entrusted since its founding with keeping the flame of art appreciation burning bright. Each year we celebrate this tradition of excellence with a gala that salutes the artists who have made Sausalito their home and the patrons that support their endeavors.

Mr. Randolph's serving as a member of the commission—let alone its chairperson—sends the wrong message to both the arts community and our citizenry. The time has come for his fellow members and all Sausalitans who value the dignity of every individual to rise up and expel this viper from our midst.

He saved the column, attached it to an email, and was about to click send when it occurred to him: hadn't he already left a message for Rob Timmons advising him that this week's column would arrive no later than noon tomorrow?

It would appear odd to submit a completed article at this time, particularly after claiming that he was otherwise engaged for the evening. Plus, while he thought he had created a compelling and well-written piece, things might look different to him in the morning. After all, "expel this viper from our midst" was perhaps a bit too strident. It was not like Warren to put himself directly in the line of fire, and there would no doubt be those who took issue with this column.

One more read tomorrow morning, and off it goes, he finally decided.

Now, it was time for more important things—open that bottle of Chianti Rufina, check the ragu, get that pasta cooking, and prepare for what he hoped would be a perfect evening.

No sooner had he savored that first careful sip of that expensive Chianti than the doorbell chimed. Warren glanced in surprise at the kitchen clock. It was only six forty-five. His guest was early, but perhaps he had gotten the time wrong.

Warren took a quick, desperate glance in the mirror. He brushed his hair back, briefly regretted his aging face, and went to open the door.

To his surprise—and discomfort—he found himself staring into the hard, angry features of Ray Sirica.

CHAPTER FIFTEEN

One of Holly's many tasks was to do a final check of editorial and advertising for each edition of *The Standard*.

Working in the office adjacent to Rob's, she called out with a warning: "We've got a hole on page fifteen! I don't have Bradley's 'Heard About Town' column for this week."

At this point in the day, Rob was busy closing up one edition and starting work on the next. He looked at his watch. Doing so brought to mind Warren's message. "He phoned last night and left a voicemail that he was going out, but would have his column in by noon today."

"But it's already close to one! I've got to upload finished page layouts to the printer in three hours if we're going to make the overnight mail drop."

Rob sighed. "Let me call him and see if he forgot to email it to us."

To his surprise, both Warren's home and cell went to voicemail.

"I can't locate him," Rob called out.

"Then how do you want me to fill the hole on page fifteen?" Holly asked, standing at the doorstep to Rob's office.

"How about if we go with a best of 'Heard About Town'?"

Holly rolled her eyes. "Rob, Bradley has no 'best of' columns."

"Ha, ha, very funny. Okay, give me a few minutes, and I'll think of something."

While Rob's mind raced through his options, this not being the first time he'd been required to make a last-minute content change, his attention drifted back to that phone message Warren left. It wasn't like him to miss a deadline. Particularly not when he called to say his column was nearly complete except for a few finishing touches.

Rob's contact with Warren was minimal—no more than an occasional phone call to discuss the column, something that Rob regularly did with others in his small group of community reporters.

His only reason for paying more attention was that Warren was one of Sausalito's more colorful characters and he had direct ties to the troublesome Alma Samuels and her Ladies of Liberty. More importantly, at the moment, his "Heard About Town" columns of the last two weeks had everyone talking about what was coming next: just the kind of buzz any weekly community newspaper publisher dreams of having.

Over the past week, every time he'd heard Warren referred to as the "Gossiping Gourmet," he smiled to himself. Since the turn of the early twentieth century, when William Randolph Hearst was told by Sausalito's ladies and gentlemen of distinction to take himself, his mistress, and his new money to another part of California, this had been a town where people famously enjoyed sitting in judgment on the private lives of others.

Paradoxically, Sausalito relished its colorful characters and any chance to gossip about their lives. Case in point: the 1960s election of the renowned, albeit retired madam, Sally Stanford, as the town's mayor. Rob loved the caricature hanging in city hall, showing Stanford smoking a cigarette as she conducted a council meeting, sitting regally under a sign that read, "No Smoking Allowed."

When Rob purchased *The Standard*, in the period before he added other weekly editions, he paid more attention to the catfighting and backbiting that moved the town's narrative forward from one year to the next. Rob was enough of a businessman to realize that Warren was good for the paper. One-half of his readers loved him and wanted to know what he was thinking, while the other half disliked him but couldn't resist finding out what was in his column. For any publisher, this was the best of both worlds.

Early that evening, with the Sausalito edition uploaded to the printer, and still no word from Bradley, Rob could not set aside his curiosity regarding Warren's disappearance. Karin was up in Corte Madera with the children at a late afternoon play date, so Rob went in search of his missing columnist.

Rob had never been to Warren's house. Still, like most Sausalito natives, Rob knew every avenue, road, street, lane, cul-de-sac, and hillside stairway in the small town.

He discovered Warren's home was the very last address on

Prospect Avenue. The substantial rains that, once every three or four years, came in December and persisted into early April could give the houses in this part of town a careworn appearance. The storms roll up and over the Marin Headlands and descend first upon an area located in the southern end of Sausalito, known to locals as "Hurricane Gulch."

To the unknowing eye, homes like Warren's cottage appear to be perched precariously on one of the area's steepest hillsides. In truth, nearly all of Sausalito sits on bedrock. The real threat to these homes comes not from earthquakes, but mudslides during a year with unusually ferocious and soaking rains.

Rob had known the previous owner, Mrs. Danvers. She was his third-grade teacher at Bayside Elementary. None of the children ever met Mr. Danvers. What little they could pick up by badgering their parents was that Mr. Danvers had died many years earlier of what was referred to in discreet whispers as a "bad heart." Based on this, it was Rob's classmate Eddie Austin's contention that Mrs. Danvers quite likely killed Mr. Danvers and disposed of his body late one night in the canyon brush below their house.

Unlike Rob, who was an A-student, Eddie had invariably brought home Cs. But his endless speculation on the demise of Mr. Danvers likely indicated a detective investigator in the making.

As Rob pulled his aging Jeep next to Warren's even older Toyota Camry, the wooden deck that served as the home's carport—an aging tangle of metal supports bolted to the steep hill below—groaned loudly. It was just past six-thirty. The headlands loomed so high over the property that the cottage had been in dark shadows for the last two hours.

The home had a system of supports, separate from the parking deck, although it appeared as though the house was sitting atop the same structure. If Rob stepped to his left, he could have walked around to the cottage's back entrance. But, of course, the proper thing to do was to turn right and walk over the crumbling walkway to Warren's front door.

It appeared that inside the home all the lights were turned off. For a small house, its doorbell was befitting a British country estate.

In a house this size, Rob thought, those chimes could wake the dead.

He waited a few moments more, but no Warren.

Rob was back at his vehicle when it occurred to him that if Warren had gone out, he most likely would have taken his car. Rob pondered for a few moments whether he wanted to snoop around the back of the cottage.

What the hell? I've come this far.

This time, as he stepped back over the creaking wood deck, he moved to his left. A sense of dread came over him that he did not fully understand. Then, he stopped suddenly. An icy chill went down his spine.

At the far end of the house, there was a porch swing, ideally positioned for sipping a morning cup of coffee while enjoying a dramatic sunrise over the East Bay. Warren sat on the far right side of the swing. He was dressed in a tweed jacket, and he was slumped just slightly against the swing's armrest.

There's little that a newsman doesn't see if he's been in the business for a decade or more, but in sleepy Sausalito and its surrounding towns, the deceased have most often been tagged, bagged, and sent on their way to the morgue before a reporter arrives.

This was not one of those times.

Functioning on a blend of determined compulsion and uneasy revulsion, Rob approached what he logically assumed was the body of Warren Bradley.

The face was not ashen but had a wax-like patina. Warren wore a white shirt. The two top buttons were open, revealing a rather dapper-looking gold ascot. Because of Warren's tweed jacket and black slacks, Rob assumed that the dead man must have requested the delay in filing his column because he had a date.

Rob imagined that Warren most likely nodded off and died peacefully in his sleep sometime later that night after he had returned home.

He must have come out on the porch for a breath of fresh air, Rob thought, perhaps to recover from one too many glasses of wine.

Warren's hands were shoved down into the pockets of his jacket, apparently to keep him warm on what was likely a chilly night in the gulch.

Dazed by his discovery, Rob walked back to his car and reached for his cell phone. Others in a panic might have called 911, but Rob had stored in his contacts the non-emergency numbers for the Sausalito Police and Fire/Rescue service. In a town with steep hills and blind curves, it would take a few minutes for both the squad car and the fire department's Emergency Medical Team to arrive, and it was evident to Rob that there was no need to rush.

CHAPTER SIXTEEN

Only moments after Rob slipped the cell phone back into his pocket, he could hear the sirens echoing through Sausalito as emergency vehicles began their journey from the bayside flats up into the hills.

There was, of course, no real cause for the sound and light show. Its only possible benefit was to remind taxpayers that their police and emergency service team were busy serving the public. The cacophony of howling dogs set off by the high-pitched noise only added to the community's sense of curiosity and excitement.

In less than a minute, half of the town was staring out windows to see what was causing the fuss. Two minutes later, the sirens whined to a halt in front of Warren's humble cottage.

Rob greeted Chief Hans Petersen, Patrol Officer Steve Hansen, and three members of the city's fire and rescue squad with handshakes all around. There was a strained professional posture Rob and Petersen struck whenever in each other's presence. Rob was continually expecting Petersen's team to stumble, and Petersen was hoping to give a longstanding critic of his work no new ammunition.

"Warren's weekly column was due at the paper no later than noon today," Rob began, knowing of the long and close relationship that Bradley had with Petersen and his officers.

"Last night, he called and left a message assuring me that he'd have his column in on time. I tried reaching him by phone several times this afternoon when the column did not appear. After I sent the Sausalito edition to the printer, I thought I'd drive up here before heading home for the night, to check up on him. I found him out here on the back porch swing."

Petersen sauntered over to where, from a distance, Warren looked like he was comfortably enjoying the evening lights coming on across the bay.

"Well, look at that! Give him a glass of Chardonnay and a plate of that dilled salmon he liked to make, and you would think he was just out here enjoying the view and taking in the evening air," Petersen said, as he circled the swing slowly.

Pompous ass! Rob thought.

"Well that's the end of those gourmet luncheons he brought us once a month," Hansen said while crouching down to study Warren's frozen face. It seemed grayer than it had appeared to Rob when he first arrived, but perhaps that was just a result of the fading daylight.

"How come Bradley never brought us any lunches? All we got was those damn pancakes for our annual benefit breakfast," EMT officer Dave Nichols asked.

"Because you couldn't tell him what was going on around town," Hansen sneered.

"Okay, knock off the bullshit, we've got work to do," Petersen barked.

"What now?" Rob asked, thinking about going home. Although sitting down to dinner seemed pointless since his appetite had vanished.

Petersen shrugged. "Given the fact that the body is colder than Santa's elves on Christmas Eve, I think it's time we get a call in to the county coroner."

Hansen went back to his squad car to call dispatch. A few minutes later, he walked back to the group, shaking his head. "There's been a crash up in Novato on 101—two fatalities. The coroner is up there now. Dispatch requested that we take the body up to the morgue since we're dealing with a pretty clear case of death by natural causes."

"Okay, boys," Nichols said to the two other members of his emergency rescue team, "Let's get Mr. Bradley on a stretcher and roll him out of here."

"Beats bagging and tagging, which is what you get when the coroner's people show up," Petersen said quietly to Rob, patting him on the shoulder.

Rob smiled and thought, for all Petersen knows Warren and I were longtime friends and colleagues. Assuming the same as Petersen—that Rob viewed Warren as a fallen comrade —Nichols wanted to remove the body in the most respectful manner possible. He came up behind the body and slid his hands under Warren's armpits and linked them together in the center of his chest.

"Grab both his feet," Nichols directed one of his crew. "We're going to lift him up and over the back of this swing." He then turned to Petersen and Hansen and said, "I'm going to need you guys to back us up. Get on either side of the body and bring the swing forward while we lift him up and out. Depending on how long he's been out here—I guess more than twelve hours—the amount of rigor mortis that has set in won't make this any easier."

Rob's throat tightened as he wondered just how gruesome this was going to get. His feet were ready to walk away, but his mind told him to stay. He was no crime reporter, but Rob wasn't the kind of journalist who only wrote a once-weekly gardening column, and he certainly didn't want to appear as such.

Just a couple of steps behind the swing, the stretcher was set up—flat, and in a lifted and locked position; Nichols took a deep breath and gave a pull. Warren was no more than five-foot eight-inches and probably one hundred and seventy pounds. Still, a body that's been sitting for that long is not easy to lift.

After a couple of tries, Nichols and his partner, Hal Michaels, decided on plan B.

"Let's lower the gurney and bring it around to the front of the swing. We'll move the body forward. At least that way, gravity will be on our side."

It was easier, particularly when they decided not to be overly concerned that the body would take a couple of bangs between sliding off the porch swing and onto the gurney. Petersen stepped in and raised the rail on the outer side of the gurney, fearful of what Rob might write if Warren's body rolled forward off the stretcher and onto the porch.

By now, twilight had turned into night. It was awkward and unnerving for Rob to watch what he realized was no easy feat. In spite of all their best efforts, Warren's body nearly missed the stretcher, but Petersen and Hansen were prepared to stop it from doing that. The commotion caused both of Warren's arms to fall free of his jacket's pockets. The EMT officers were too busy steadying the body on the stretcher and preparing to strap it down to notice the curious sight that caused Petersen to bark out, *"What the hell?"* while he was in the middle of rhapsodizing to Rob over his two favorite Warren Bradley dishes.

Petersen pulled a flashlight out of Hansen's equipment belt, who turned to see what had captured his boss's attention. The flashlight illuminated the bottom of Warren's right sleeve. It hung there, several inches below Warren's arm as if he were a child in an oversized coat.

Now that Petersen had everyone's attention, he walked around the stretcher. On the opposite side of the gurney he ran the flashlight up to look inside Warren's left jacket sleeve.

"Okay, everyone freeze," Petersen declared. "We're standing in the middle of a crime scene. I'm sure we've already contaminated it, so let's step away from the body and give this a little thought."

"What are you talking about, Chief?" Nichols asked.

"Let me put it to you directly: *when people die of natural causes, they get to keep both their hands*—something Mr. Bradley here has lost."

After slipping on a pair of blue nitrile gloves, Petersen pushed up Bradley's sleeves.

Rob could not believe what he was seeing, but it was true. Both of Warren Bradley's hands were missing.

Over the next few hours, all the usual things that happen at a crime scene occurred.

While the thought briefly occurred to Petersen to put the body back on the porch swing as close to the pose it was in when they arrived on the scene, that seemed impractical, particularly considering Rob was standing nearby watching their every move.

Why me, God? Petersen thought. His retirement was scheduled for late October, less than six months away.

More Sausalito police cars arrived, as well as two from the sheriff's department. One carried Eddie Austin.

Finally, a little after ten, the coroner arrived. Several times Petersen explained how the missing hands had gone unnoticed until the body was placed onto the stretcher. Each time he retold the story it was received with a shake of the head and a look of surprise from both Eddie and the coroner.

Shortly after eleven, Bradley's body was finally on its way to the morgue, and his small cottage was wrapped with yellow CRIME SCENE tape.

In the thick brush below Bradley's home, a coyote wandering through the canyon came upon Warren's missing hands. The animal had been attracted by the subtle scent of sausage and porcini ragu with just a hint of a mixed fruit cobbler. In little time this lean, hungry beast devoured all but a few scraps of critical evidence and then moved on.

Those spare bits of flesh and bone—all that remained of the famous chef's two talented hands—were carried off at daybreak by a vulture patrolling the hills of Sausalito searching for unexpected treats.

CHAPTER SEVENTEEN

That night, Rob and Karin slept only four hours, having stayed up until two in the morning discussing the bizarre details of Warren Bradley's murder.

In the hope that the fresh air might revive his tired mind, Rob walked down to his office, located in an old Victorian on Princess Street, just three blocks beyond the hub of the city's tourist center.

Rob steeled himself for what he knew would be the first of several long days. It was Wednesday, and *The Sausalito Standard* would arrive in homes in a few hours. What would be missing from this edition was likely destined to be this year's biggest story.

"Damn it," Rob repeatedly mumbled to himself with his hands shoved into the pockets of a light tweed sports jacket. He remained oblivious to the birds chirping their greeting to a lovely blue morning and the sun rising over the hills of the East Bay. Among other things, Bradley's killer was undoubtedly guilty of lousy timing. Rob knew, however, that this was the unavoidable reality in publishing a weekly newspaper, particularly in an age of instant communication. Just as it is with any endeavor, luck and timing play a significant role.

Having been the person who discovered Bradley's body, this simple reality was particularly painful. *The Sausalito Standard's* lead story this week was: "Parks and Recreation Commission Reviews Plans for Proposed Improvements to Dunphy Park."

Not nearly the conversation starter he would have had with a headline like: "Sausalito Columnist Warren Bradley Found Murdered."

Rob knew, however, he had to focus on getting out the rest of *The Standard's* other weekly editions. At the same time, he couldn't help but wonder when the county's daily newspaper, *The Independent*, would send a reporter to cover Bradley's murder.

There was, however, a silver lining. The dailies, the local TV anchors, and radio newscasters no doubt would be all over the Bradley story for the next twenty-four hours. Afterward, there would be another dramatic story to cover: A body found floating in the bay; a politician found with someone else's spouse, money, or both; perhaps a bank heist, or a traffic pile up on the Richardson Bridge.

By next week's local edition of *The Standard*, he'd be the only reporter covering the Bradley murder investigation—

And that story would continue to hold his local readers' attention, at least until it was brought to a resolution.

Depending on how the investigation unfolded, Bradley's slaying could be *The Standard's* top story for weeks to come, and local readers would be waiting anxiously for their community weekly to arrive with the only detailed and ongoing coverage of this story.

When Rob dragged his tired body and frazzled mind up the long narrow steps to his offices on the Victorian's second floor, Holly was already there waiting breathlessly for him.

"Good God you're here early."

"I called Karin. She told me you were already on your way down here. I tried your cell when I heard about Warren, but you didn't pick up. Karin told me you were there—and that you saw the body! How cool is that? Pretty gruesome, huh?"

"Who told you Bradley was killed?"

"One of my neighbors. I ran into her as I was going across the street to pick up some bread and eggs to make for my breakfast. She'd heard it from two cops on Bridgeway. She passes them every morning on their way down to Café Divino for their morning lattes and bagels." Holly's brown eyes were twinkling, and her short black curly hair bounced up and down as she talked. She was as excited as a kid on the first day of summer vacation.

Rob knew she'd never been a fan of Warren's. Every time she mentioned his name, it came with a descriptive, most often, "that mean, sneaky little man." Nor had she ever been a fan of his column. But to Holly and Rob—and most likely nearly all longtime residents—the mystery surrounding Warren's death would quickly turn the gossiping gourmet into the community's top celebrity.

One of *The Standard's* two phone lines began to ring. Seconds later, the other started. Rob's cell phone started to vibrate, and then Holly's cell phone went off as well.

"It's going to be a long day," Holly said as she rushed to answer one of the calls.

In the first couple of hours, their phones never ceased. The one voice Rob was happy to hear was that of Eddie Austin.

"So you've been assigned to the case?"

Eddie snorted. "Duh, yeah."

"Can you stop up at the office?"

"Yep. In fact, I'm two minutes away. I've got a few questions for you. Right now, you're my number one suspect."

Rob's throat went dry. "Me?"

"Sure, buddy! You had motive *and* opportunity. Bradley wrote a lousy column, and you wanted to get rid of him. It happens all the time in your business. You dirty rat!"

"Very funny," Rob mumbled. "I'm a lot of things, but a killer is not one of them."

"Relax! It's just a working theory. It's not like we're ready to issue a warrant for your arrest," Eddie laughed before clicking off.

Although Rob and Eddie grew up just blocks apart and saw each other regularly throughout their time at Bayside Elementary School, it wasn't until they both won spots on Tam High's junior varsity basketball team that they became inseparable.

Their parents always laughed about the fact that they had mirror image families. Rob had a sister, Lisa, who was two years his junior. Eddie had an older sister— Andrea, who was two years his senior.

They were born one week apart, with Eddie being the older with a late July birthday. Although they went their separate ways at San Francisco State—Rob into journalism and Eddie into criminal justice—the two stayed very close. In fact, Eddie served as Rob's best man when he married Karin, and Rob was Eddie's best man when he married Sharon.

Eddie's parents, like Rob's, chose a different place than Sausalito to retire. Rob's parents headed south to San Diego, whereas Eddie's parents headed north, retiring in Spokane, Washington, where Eddie's mom had grown up.

Usually, at the end of a long workweek, they'd meet for beers at the town's neighborhood dive bar, Smitty's. There, Eddie and Rob, often with Holly joining them, would joke about some of the "small-minded nitwits" who too often dominated their hometown's daily chatter.

Local politics alone provided them, and the town as a whole, with their theater of the absurd. For decades, the town's city council had been a source of jokes and wonderment throughout the county. Fights broke out regularly among councilmembers, often during public meetings. Actual physical injuries were rare, but feuds were frequent and could last a decade or longer. After one of these fights, Rob, in a *Standard* editorial, labeled Sausalito "Baghdad by the Bay," which became an oft-repeated joke that generated laughs for months afterward.

Most assumed that at least three or four of the city's five councilmembers were taking money or other favors in exchange for their votes. One development project, for a small bed and breakfast establishment for example, would sail through the planning process and win council approval, to be followed six months later with an all but identical project being killed in committee.

It became common knowledge that a project, which could be anything from opening a new tourist trinket shop to the building of a mega hillside home, would fare better in the hands of one of the council majority's favored architects, attorneys, or real estate agents. This and more helped to reinforce Sausalito's reputation as "the meanest little town in the west."

But, for all the in-fighting, nasty gossip, adulterous affairs, viciously thrown insults, and occasionally thrown punches, murder was a rare occurrence in Sausalito.

Most of Eddie's homicides came from the few pockets of poverty and crime in the county. In the towns *The Standard* covered—Sausalito, Belvedere, Tiburon, Mill Valley, Larkspur, Corte Madera, Kentfield, and Ross—people might have expressed a desire to kill their neighbors, but acting on that impulse was extremely rare. The last homicide investigation in Sausalito was several years earlier. It ended quickly when a jealous lover confessed to what she described as "a crime of passion." She ran over her adulterous husband in the family's steep driveway, which she first claimed to be "a tragic accident."

Eddie was still chuckling to himself as he entered *The Standard*'s offices.

Despite the deadline to prep tomorrow's edition of the Mill Valley paper, which was due at the printers by four that afternoon, Rob and Holly were eager to hear any news Eddie might bring.

"I'll tell you two, right up front—this case is going to take awhile," Eddie claimed with certainty.

Rob was pleased to hear that, hoping the Bradley case would boost readership for weeks to come. "If you're right about that," Rob began with a smile, "then the Ladies of Liberty —also known as the nearly deaf and almost dead—are going to go wild. Warren was their poster boy! They'll be organizing protests outside of Sausalito police headquarters, demanding answers. More importantly, demanding an arrest."

"Like I care," Eddie retorted with a laugh. "The sheriff's offices are in Marin City, and up in San Rafael. Your fair ladies won't be showing up in either of those locations anytime soon. Come on, admit it, Rob. A headache for Chief Petersen is usually entertainment for you."

Holly's eyes opened wide. "Don't those clowns have some clues as to who may have killed that nasty old gossipmonger?"

"Hey, watch that, Holly. I'm working the Bradley case too. I'm on loan from the sheriff's office to the Sausalito PD until they can clear this case. Right now, I'm included in that group of 'clowns' without clues." At the thought of working closely with the Sausalito PD, Eddie shook his head. "To be honest, there's not a hell of a lot of evidence at the murder scene and it certainly is an oddball case! The twist of Bradley's missing hands, if nothing else, are going to make this an ongoing story.

"Rob finds old walrus puss on his porch swing, enjoying a bit of fresh air. The only thing wrong is that he's cold as ice. The guy is seventy-two, perhaps a little on the young side for a fatal stroke or heart attack, but certainly nothing out of the ordinary. Petersen and the EMT boys can't get the county coroner, so they're happy to take him up to the morgue and get back to their coffee maker, donuts, and computer games. Then we hit a snag—the nicely dressed gentleman's two arms end just above his wrists. No hands. So, where are the hands?"

Rob and Holly, transfixed by Eddie's retelling of the facts, merely shook their heads and shrugged their shoulders.

"We can't find any hands, and we've got four of Sausalito's finest—I use that term loosely— looking for them. As we speak, they're walking through that thick brush under Bradley's house."

Holly, who could never resist a pun, jumped in and said, "I'd be happy to lend you a hand, but my day job keeps me pretty busy."

"Somehow, Holly, I knew you couldn't resist saying that," Eddie declared with a smile.

"Why was there no blood?" Holly asked. "I've got to figure that getting your hands whacked off would cause a bloody mess."

"The theory we're working on now is that Bradley was suffocated, most likely with a pillow, shortly after midnight," Eddie explained. "In all likelihood, the killer spent twenty or thirty minutes rummaging through his place looking for something, then wiped the whole place clean of any prints. Our working theory is after he did all that, he decided to take Bradley's hands as a souvenir. Or maybe, he didn't want us to have his victim's fingerprints. I already checked and found there are no prints for Bradley on file. Now, remember, Rob, all this happened approximately nineteen hours before you went to check on him. But, as far as blood, Holly, dead people don't bleed."

"Of course!" Holly said pushing Rob's arm with her elbow. "I should have known that from all the murder mysteries I read."

"When the heart stops pumping, the blood that flows out of us quits soon after. It's not much time before it turns into a thick goop and stays inside the arteries and veins. You can get some leakage, depending on gravity and the position of the body, but that's about it. In all likelihood, Bradley's hands were cut off thirty minutes or longer after he died. And in Bradley's house, the gourmet chef that he was, there were several utensils that could've done the job. Most likely it was..." Eddie paused and flipped open his notepad, "...a Victorinox Forschner Rosewood meat cleaver, which we assume the killer found where he left it, sitting on the kitchen counter. It looked spotless, but it was one of many items we bagged for the lab team to take a closer look at."

"*Eww!* Kind of like scalping him, only different!" Holly's eyes opened wide.

She sat down at her computer. In a moment, her screen filled with the cleaver maker's product description, which she enthusiastically read aloud: "'A high carbon stainless steel blade made to the highest standards by expertly trained Swiss craftsmen. This product is ideal for cutting through joints and bones.' *Double eww!*"

"You're enjoying this a little too much," Rob muttered. But from his grin, he seemed just as amused as annoyed.

"I'll tell you this much," Eddie continued, "This killer was no amateur. A whack job, for sure, but not a sloppy one. If his only aim was to kill Bradley, suffocation potentially leaves no telltale signs. Unless there was a struggle, there's a reasonable chance he would have gotten away with it. The house shows no sign of a fight and no sign of forced entry. That being said, the hands were taken as souvenirs. Or, perhaps in a brief death struggle, Bradley scratched the arms of his assailant. Skin or fiber evidence can be hard to completely clean out from under fingernails, so you could argue that the killer wanted to walk away with what might have been critical evidence."

"Maybe the hands were taken as a cult thing, or maybe it's a warning," Holly reasoned.

Rob and Eddie exchanged glances. They could tell Holly loved playing the role of junior detective.

"Or maybe someone was angry enough about some of the columns Bradley wrote that they cut off his hands as an act of revenge," Holly continued. "Those hands of Bradley's could be hanging as souvenirs in someone's home at this very moment, right here in Sausalito," she added with an obvious sense of growing excitement.

"Let's not forget that the killer took the time to make his victim quite presentable. He propped him up on the porch swing like a department store mannequin," Eddie replied. "So unless the killer had someone else there to help, we're dealing with an individual with a respectable degree of strength."

"Wow. This is going to stir up some crazy stuff," Rob declared with obvious excitement. "Just imagine, Holly, the increased ad sales for the paper if this case remains unsolved for weeks! This might turn out to be the best thing that blabbermouth ever did for this newspaper!"

"You're right, Rob" Holly admitted with a mischievous grin. "But you probably don't want to put that thought into print."

CHAPTER EIGHTEEN

I t was increasingly difficult for Rob to keep his focus on news stories such as "Remodeled Children's Section of the Mill Valley Library Announced," or "Ross Common Landscaping Budget Dispute Enters Second Month." As he anticipated, Sausalito was in a twist over the Bradley murder.

By Friday afternoon, less than seventy-two hours after the discovery of Warren's body, Alma sent a letter to *The Standard*, co-signed by each member of the Ladies of Liberty, demanding increased funding for the Bradley investigation.

"One of our community's most distinguished citizens has been cut down in his prime," she wrote. "We are bereft at the loss of a charming and gifted neighbor. Can we honestly believe that any of us are safe in our homes while this deranged killer remains at large? Dark and menacing forces must not be allowed to envelop our peaceful corner of a troubled world!"

Borrowing from Shakespeare, Alma concluded, "This case

of murder most foul must be guided to a swift and satisfactory conclusion by the joint efforts of our police and civic leaders! Their actions now will reassure us, or deprive us, of the confidence and trust we have placed in them."

"Wow," Holly said to Rob while reading over his shoulder. "'Cut down in his prime?' He was over seventy! Maybe she meant prime in tortoise years. We've got no shortage of reader comments for the letters section this week. Half of our writers want to know why the cops haven't arrested Grant Randolph."

"I've probably got to run a couple of them," Rob said. "But I don't want to add to the hysteria by running a page worth of letters calling for Randolph's arrest. The thing that worries me, even more, is right now we don't have much of a story beyond what the dailies have covered over the past two days."

Just about everyone in Sausalito—except the police—had a theory about Bradley's slaying.

Eddie had theories as well. But because his job was to deal in fact, not mere supposition, he found himself on a frustrating ride that, at least to this point, was taking him nowhere.

As was their custom, every Friday after work he, Rob, and Holly ended their week with a drink at Smitty's. Together, they'd have a couple of drinks and toast the start of the coming weekend.

They weren't in much danger of being overheard. It was a quiet time of day inside the poorly lit bar, which catered on late weekday afternoons mostly to ancient mariners and long-time Sausalito residents who preferred to share a drink in the company of familiar faces as opposed to the myriad of day visitors who patronized the few bars on Bridgeway. In every sense, Smitty's lived up to its reputation as a neighborhood dive bar, and its patrons liked it that way.

While Smitty's was half empty in the late afternoon, in another four hours, it would be packed and pulsing to old-fashioned rock 'n roll blaring from a jukebox. The place had the permanent scent of beer, sweat, cheap perfume, and aftershave.

Noting that Rob was already there but alone, Eddie asked, "Where's your partner in crime?"

"Told me she had a date and rushed out the door at four-thirty. I never complain when she wants out a little early on a Friday. Most days she's already at her desk working before I get into the office around eight."

"She's a keeper, Rob," Eddie said, lifting his Guinness beer in salute.

"Any progress with the Bradley case?" Rob asked as he raised his Guinness as well and tapped Eddie's.

"Not much. Some plausible theories about the time and sequence of the murder, but killer and motive, all pretty slim at this point." Shaking his head, Eddie grimaced in frustration.

"I'd love to come up with something more than what the dailies had over the last week."

As Rob anticipated, for the San Francisco media the story had already lost its allure. If not for the gruesome detail that the victim was missing both his hands, the story would have died in less than twenty-four hours. But now, with nothing new to report, the story was sitting quietly on the back burner, awaiting an arrest.

After a long, thoughtful pause, Eddie said, "We've got some

interesting pieces, but we don't know at this point how they fit into the bigger picture."

"Like what?"

"It might not be of help, but it's certainly of interest. Bradley had at least two guests the night he died. One was Ray Sirica."

"Whoa! That's Randolph's pal! You know, the one who wrote that great letter to *The Standard* complaining about Bradley. I loved it when he called Warren out as 'the gossiping gourmet.' It certainly gave Holly and me a good laugh."

"That's the guy," Eddie said. "I can only imagine the stir that letter would have continued to cause if Bradley had not been dispatched to that great culinary institute in the sky."

"So, who spotted Ray Sirica?"

"Around six-forty-five on Monday evening, one of Bradley's neighbors was walking his dog. He recognized Ray as he drove by and followed the car down to the end of Prospect as it pulled into Bradley's carport."

"How did you hear about this?"

"I worked the neighbors for anything of interest. You never know when someone sees something that they think is nothing but it turns out to be something; or, they want to keep a low profile, so they get nervous about calling in a tip, which is often the case in a murder investigation."

"You think it might be a break in the case?" Rob asked eagerly.

"No, news hawk, but it's something. When you don't have much to go on, you're happy to follow any scrap of information that's thrown your way."

"Having been there the night of the murder, did Sirica come forward to the police?"

"No. I went looking for him. I spoke with him Thursday afternoon at his home. He seemed a little uneasy. But I could see why. He goes up to plead with Bradley, as he explained, in the hope of getting Grant Randolph out of his crosshairs. You know, the old 'can't you find anyone else to write about.' The next thing Sirica knows, Bradley is found murdered."

"But you think there's no chance Sirica is your guy?"

"The timing is way off. A neighbor who was putting out the trash around nine-thirty that night saw the lights on at Bradley's place. A door or window must have been open because he's confident he heard voices and the sound of Bradley laughing. One more reason—Sirica's story holds up that he spoke to Warren for ten minutes, got nowhere, and left. It seems pretty doubtful that Warren invited Sirica to stay for dinner and the two shared a lovely evening together. So this begs the question: Who was Sausalito's gossiping gourmet entertaining the night he died?"

"I agree with you. It's unlikely it was Sirica," Rob said with a short laugh. "Does Sirica suspect his buddy, Randolph?"

"He didn't say, but by the way he flinched when I spoke of Randolph, I think it's pretty likely the thought has crossed Sirica's mind. Then again, half the pinheads in town think Randolph killed Bradley, particularly after the public confrontation they had at Sausalito's nutty night at the opera."

"Trust me; if Karin and I knew that confrontation was going to happen, we would have gone in spite of the music."

Eddie snorted. "You and me both! By the way, and keep this to yourself for now, I learned from Sirica that Randolph and his wife flew to New York City Wednesday morning, hours after you discovered Warren's body."

"Wow, wait until Alma and her pals hear about that."

"I don't think that will take too long to get out there. News, good or bad, travels pretty fast in this town, with or without the help of your newspaper's late columnist."

"Well, they're not going to like hearing Grant Randolph slipped out of town."

"That's fine with me. While Alma's brigade is out there chasing shadows, I've got to stay focused on the facts of this case."

"What else?" Rob asked with a hint of desperation in his voice.

"Right now I—and our friends at the Sausalito PD—have little more than that. It's not all that surprising. Bradley's house is at the very end of a poorly lit street and the sight lines into his place stink, making it more difficult than usual to get information out of Sausalito's usually nosey neighbors." Eddie leaned in. "There is one other thing, however. The Marin County Medical Examiner, Max Brownstein, suspects death by suffocation, and it's highly probable the old boy never knew what hit him. Most often, when a person has a pillow held over their face, there will be signs of a struggle, such as bruising to the victim's cheeks and mouth, perhaps even a broken nose, if the killer has to apply enough pressure to subdue a struggling victim. Most commonly, there is DNA in the form of skin and hair from the killer under the victim's fingernails—evidence we obviously lack with Warren's hands having vanished. Additionally, Bradley's face doesn't show any bruising, which means he was sound asleep, drunk, or most likely both, when he was murdered."

"What will you do about Randolph?"

"For now, we'll keep him on our radar. In the old west, a dispute like the one he had with Bradley might have ended in a gunfight. Today, it ends when both parties grow tired of exchanging insults. Or they get tired of paying their attorneys to exchange insults for them."

Rob was still hoping for something he could lead with for the coming week's coverage of Bradley's slaying. To loosen Eddie's tongue a little more, Rob said, "Let me get you another beer."

Eddie happily agreed.

When two more beers were delivered, Rob toasted, "To murder most foul!"

Eddie nodded and smiled. "Even minus the victim's hands, these aren't usual circumstances we're dealing with. No facial wounds or contusions, that's also pretty surprising. But there was a notably elevated blood alcohol level in Warren's body; enough to indicate that he had drunk a good amount shortly before his death. Of course, the two empty bottles of Chianti on the kitchen counter pretty much told us that. It's possible that the suffocation was forceful enough and the victim was in a deep enough sleep that it was over pretty quickly. Let me put it this way, if Warren did become aware he was being suffocated, it was likely in the last few moments of his life."

"Could there have been any fibers from the bedding inside his mouth or nostrils?" Rob asked.

"A swab for fibers inside the nose or mouth is pretty inconclusive. Most mornings, all of us have a fair number of fibers on our lips, noses, and mouths from our bedding, we just are unaware of that. Obviously if there was a real struggle there would have been more fibers, but just as the lack of bruising to the face reveals, it appears as though there was little if any struggle. Given Warren's age and his level of intoxication that's all plausible."

"So, right now you're saying every road leads to a dead end?"

"Not at all. But in the absence of the kind of physical evidence that would make this an easier crime to solve, a good investigator has to start constructing scenarios based on plausible theories. Call it the Sherlock Holmes method. What's at the murder scene that we're not considering at the moment?"

"Are you boys discussing murder without me?"

Both Eddie and Rob turned around to find Holly standing behind them. She was holding her usual drink—a vodka martini.

"I'm surprised to see you here," Rob said. "I thought you had a hot date."

"So did I, but the jerk called me just as I got to the bar at Poggio's to say that he couldn't make it. What's a girl to do? So I thought I'd come over here and see what you two were talking about."

Holly grabbed a chair from the empty table behind her and sat down. "Are you chatting about our dearly departed gossiping gourmet? I hope so! I need something to cheer me up."

"What is it with you and murder?" Rob asked.

"Look, I've read Sue Grafton from A to Y! Maybe I'll have something to contribute here," Holly said as she took a dainty sip followed by a less dainty gulp of her martini and then leaned in conspiratorially. "So, are you closing the circle, tightening the noose, and preparing to check Warren's killer into the gray bar hotel?"

Eddie laughed. "Who do you think you are, Sausalito's answer to Nancy Drew?"

"Nope. I'm just a girl hoping to enjoy a cocktail with a side of murder late on a Friday afternoon. So come on Eddie, spill! Poor Warren's soul is calling out for justice. Who put an end to that miserable weasel's existence?"

"Not a fan, I assume?" Eddie said with a raised eyebrow.

"Not by a longshot!"

"I was just explaining to Rob that we've got some good theories—always an important first step in tracking down a killer when all the obvious clues are not there."

"Goody." Having reached the end of her drink, Holly waved at Gladys, their usual waitress, while pointing to her empty glass.

"Hangar 1 Vodka, two olives and one onion," Holly called out.

Gladys rolled her eyes. "I know, Holly, I know!"

"Sounds like you're here more than once every Friday," Eddie said teasingly.

"It's not that! I'm just a better tipper than you two tightwads."

The proof of her claim was in how quickly Holly's drink appeared. "Here you go, doll, just the way you like it," Gladys assured her.

Rob and Eddie exchanged knowing glances.

Holly grinned. "What can I say? She's a fast learner."

Rob sighed. "So, Eddie, what kind of scenarios are you considering?"

"Let's go back to what we logically know: high-quality meat cleaver or not, an elderly arthritic is not going around whacking off the hands of their murder victims."

"What does that tell ya?" Holly asked as she sucked on an olive.

"For starters, it tells us that over half of Sausalito's population did not commit this crime."

That brought a shared snort of laughter from both Rob and Holly.

"Let's keep the obvious front and center. In life, Warren was around a hundred and sixty-five pounds, and about five-foot-eight. Dead bodies that size would require a pretty strong guy to move them around. And from the point Bradley was suffocated and laid out on the floor, where it's reasonable to assume that he had his hands chopped off, and then—"

Holly was just about to say something, when Eddie jumped in and said, "Wait for it," shaking his finger back and forth. "... dressed, or at least cleaned up, carried outside, placed and posed on the back porch swing. It's likely our killer is a male, with a strong back and in pretty good shape. I suspect he frequents the gym and has a particular fondness for strength-building exercises."

"I imagine you know that Grant Randolph is a pretty healthy forty-something," Holly said. "I was at one of those open houses for the artist's co-op down at the Marinship, and I saw him. Tight waist, broad shoulders, big arms. I mean, hubba hubba! He Tarzan, me Jane."

"I get the feeling you were impressed by Commissioner Randolph's physique?" Rob asked teasingly.

"You bet I was," Holly declared. Perching at the very edge of her chair, she turned back to Eddie and asked, "So, knowing that, where do you go from here?"

"I'll tell you this much, Holly: If Grant Randolph was his killer, he's a real whack job to murder Bradley at a time when he would instantly be suspect numero uno. The first thing I did was a pretty detailed background check on Randolph through the NYPD database. No priors and no record of him being involved in physical altercations of any sort. He might be physically capable of hurting Bradley, but that doesn't mean he did."

"That's good news," Holly agreed. "I would hate to see people like Alma and her crowd be right for once in their lives. If they could, they'd string him up today."

"Sounds like you're right, Eddie, this one's not going to be easy," Rob said, finishing up the last of his beer.

"I'm afraid not; it's probably going to be a long slog, but we're going to have to dig a lot deeper into Bradley's life and learn something about everyone he knew. Remember, the one saving grace in a murder investigation is the vast majority of victims knew their killer." Deep in thought, Eddie folded his cocktail napkin in half and then added, "We have no evidence of a break-in. Warren's place was neat as a pin. Bradley didn't own much outside of his fancy cookware and utensils, and none of his possessions appear to be missing. We found his wallet in the top drawer of his bedroom dresser with one hundred and twenty dollars inside. And there was an old but rather pricey watch sitting next to it."

"Nothing of value was taken? How about his hands?" Holly chirped.

"Yes, the hands," Eddie said. He looked as if he was about to say something more, but stopped.

Silence sat uncomfortably between the three friends.

Rob and Holly looked at each other, then asked in unison: "And the hands?"

Eddie shrugged. "It may have been a diversion. Whoever killed Warren wanted to make some kind of statement. Propping him up on that back porch swing was part of that statement."

"Or maybe," Rob said slowly, "it was a warning."

"Warning?" Holly asked. "About what?"

He shook his head. "I don't know, maybe a mob thing like, 'Keep your hands to yourself,' or something?"

Holly frowned. "What do you think he did, stole a box of family recipes from some mob guy?"

"As long as I have you two master sleuths here, I want to bring up something else," Eddie said as he leaned in closer.

"We're all ears," Holly said as she and Rob inched their chairs in even closer.

"One of the items we took from Bradley's place was his laptop."

"Do the cops usually do that?" Holly asked.

"It's pretty standard, given that people keep so much information on their computers. We would have looked at his smartphone, too, if he'd had one, to check his calendar. All he had was an ancient flip phone. Anyway, we hoped he kept a calendar on his computer. The program was there, but he never used it. His cell phone had no numbers, either going in or out, that we could not identify—except for two. Both of those calls were made from pay phones in Sausalito. We got his home phone's records as well. All the numbers in and out have been identified and cleared. You guys wouldn't believe how many calls went back and forth between Alma Samuels and Bradley, not to mention some of the others in her clique—Bea Snyder, Robin Mitchell—all the usual suspects."

"It was pretty obvious that Warren was their errand boy," Holly said with a chuckle. "I imagine that's where he got a good part of the gossip that found its way into his cell phone."

"What about the pay phone calls he received?" Rob asked.

"One was from that small grocery store at the south end of Caledonia Street. The other came from the Bridgeway Café. There are only a handful of those old pay phones left in town. It's merely guesswork at this time, but I think there's a reasonable chance that the killer made both of those calls. One of them was made to Warren's cell early on the afternoon of the day he was killed. The other call came in one week earlier."

"That's interesting," Holly said hanging on Eddie's every word.

"Warren planned a dinner for two the night he was killed. It appears that the killer did not attempt to remove the evidence that he had a guest that evening. The dishes had all been washed and put in the drainer. Unless Bradley used two wine glasses, two plates, two forks and so on, Warren was not alone for his last supper."

"Does it add up to anything?" Rob asked, desperately hoping for a story angle.

"Not yet, Rob. But it helps us construct some interesting theories, such as the killer was probably not an amateur—and at the very least, no dummy, either. Murders that are the result of, say, an argument, are never as methodical as this. Crimes of passion are pretty sloppy. If the killer used a pay phone, my guess is that he or she knew that after Bradley turned up dead, checking phone records would be one of the first things an investigator was certain to do."

"Maybe the killer's cell wasn't working. If so, a pay phone was the only alternative," Holly suggested.

"Sure, that's possible. But, most phones today can go months, or even years, without receiving a call from a public pay phone. Bradley got two a week apart—and one of those two calls hours before his murder."

"Why would that matter?" Rob asked.

"If we're correct and Warren knew his killer, and since both pay phone calls originated in Sausalito, the killer probably lives, works, or both, somewhere near here."

"This is all speculation," Holly said, looking disappointedly at her now-empty glass.

"Absolutely," Eddie said. "Unless you have a killer who staples a business card to their victim's sleeve, that's where you need to begin. In the absence of actionable evidence—like prints, tissue samples under a victim's fingernails, DNA left on tossed paper napkins or tissues, and so on—educated guess-work is where the investigative process begins."

"What about the laptop? What did you find there?" Rob asked.

"Remember when you told me that Bradley left a phone message about his column being late, but he was confident he'd have it to you well before the next day's deadline? Well, here it is," Eddie said as he pulled a folded sheet of paper from his inside jacket pocket.

Rob's eyes widened as he opened Warren's final "Heard About Town" column.

"Oh, my God! I've got to see this!" Holly said as she jumped up and ran behind Rob to look over his shoulder.

Both of them read the column in silent amazement:

"In the past two weeks, much has been said about the behavior of Sausalito Fine Arts Commission chair, Grant Randolph. His arrest by police, on suspicion of spousal abuse, has no doubt shocked many in our quiet, tight-knit community...."

Both Rob and Holly were transfixed by Warren's final assault on Randolph—right through to its closing line in which he suggested that it was time for Grant's fellow art commissioners "who value the dignity of every individual to rise up and expel this viper from our midst."

As usual, it was Holly who first broke their silence. "Wow, the guy could really write when he put his mind to it!"

"What was the computer time stamp on this piece?" Rob asked.

"His last save of that document came at six-thirty-nine on the night he was killed."

"Maybe he called Randolph for comment, and he came up to the house and murdered him," Holly suggested, and then quickly added, "If they lock Randolph up and throw away the key, I wouldn't mind being his cellmate."

"Not so fast, Miss Drew," Eddie said. "As I told Rob before you arrived, it's pretty unlikely that Randolph shared dinner and two bottles of wine with Bradley before cutting off the hands that had used a computer keyboard to torment him."

Holly, who by now was three martinis into her evening and feeling no pain, picked up her bag. "Eddie, you've got your theory, and I've got mine."

As they watched her exit, Eddie turned to Rob and said, "Holly is such a great character. Don't you think she fits in perfectly with all the other wing nuts in this town?"

"The question now is," Rob added, "which one of those wing nuts, besides Grant Randolph, wanted Warren Bradley dead?"

CHAPTER NINETEEN

Earlier on Friday, Alma Samuels made a surprise telephone call to Rob. In truth, they both knew she did everything she could to pretend he and *The Standard* didn't exist beyond Warren's "Heard About Town" column. All the more reason for Rob's shock when he picked up his phone and found Alma on the line.

"Poor dear Warren's memorial service begins at ten o'clock sharp, Saturday morning," she said, without so much as a simple salutation. "I know he meant a great deal to you—or I should say, to *The Standard*. Heavens! If not for his column, I presume there would be no reason at all for your paper to exist! That being said, I presume you'll want to speak at Warren's memorial service."

Rob's first instinct was to reply in a fake voice, "Sorry, you must get wrong number," and hang up. But, he resisted temptation.

Saturday was his one morning to sleep in—a once weekly gift to himself—but he knew it would needlessly offend Alma's army if he declined the offer. He winced at the thought of attending a Ladies of Liberty arranged farewell to their dearly departed hero, but there was no graceful way to turn down the invitation. Besides, this was a rare opportunity to prove to his detractors that he was a responsible and established voice in what is often a discordant community.

"Yes," he muttered wearily, "I'd be happy to do that. I'll see you—"

Alma hung up before Rob completed his acceptance.

F riday night, after Smitty's and after dinner, Rob hastily wrote down some brief comments regarding his late columnist. He then read them to Karin as she washed and dried the dishes.

"Whatever you want to say is fine, dear," Karin said. He realized she was paying little attention to his carefully crafted words. "Honestly, Rob, the guy always gave me the creeps. The way he went around getting into everybody's business, exchanging pot roasts and cheese plates for gossip! You know, it wouldn't surprise me if he knew a little too much for his own good. My mother always told me that nosy people are likely to get their noses cut off."

Later on, when they both were in bed, Karin turned to Rob and said, "Maybe that's why the killer chopped off his hands. It could have been a warning to others to be careful about what they put into print."

"Eddie and I talked about that. Of course, Eddie thinks if that was the case, I might be the next one to lose my hands."

"I hope not," Karin said as she softly held and kissed Rob's hand. "Who would give my neck a rub after a long day with the kids?"

Both shared a good laugh as they turned out their lights. But they also wondered in silence whether they had remembered to lock the back door.

Rob had almost drifted off to sleep when he remembered something Eddie had said at Smitty's: "Nearly all victims know their killers."

The idea was worrisome enough to keep Rob awake for another hour staring into the darkness.

Warren Bradley's memorial service was held at the old Presbyterian Church at the top of Excelsior Lane, just two blocks uphill from *The Standard*'s office. It's an intimate, aging, wood structure with a small town, Thomas Kinkade-like fantasy look about it.

The crowd that turned out was large enough that a third of the mourners—those who arrived after nine-thirty—had to watch the service on two aging video monitors in the church's basement reception hall.

The Ladies of Liberty led the effort to make the service memorable. Ethel and Marilyn were in charge of floral arrangements and musical interludes. Bea and Robin assembled the potluck brunch reception to follow the service. Tissue boxes were placed discreetly throughout the church, along with enlarged pictures of Warren: stirring a sauce, pulling a roast out of the oven, decorating a cake, decanting a bottle of wine, and posing over his laptop's keyboard ready to strike.

Sausalito is a small community. In New York, Dallas, Los

Angeles, and a dozen other cities, a killer can vanish into a crowd. But that's far harder to do in a small town. And that was why Eddie is here, Rob reasoned.

Rob had just stepped up to the dais when he noticed Holly tucking herself into a small space by the church's door. Her eyelids were half closed. She too was not accustomed to being up at this hour on a Saturday. Rob was now certain that his associate editor had become a dogged amateur sleuth.

"Warren Bradley brought something special into our lives," Rob began, not at all sure what that "something special" was. "His loss leaves a void that will not be easily filled."

Rob noticed Alma and the rest of the Ladies of Liberty dabbing the corners of their eyes with lace handkerchiefs while nodding approvingly. He had long been accustomed to their disapproving glances every year at Sausalito City Hall's annual holiday season gathering, or, individually, as they passed him on the street and pretended not to notice him. At last year's annual July 4th community picnic, they closely observed Rob and Karin as they passed by with their two small children in tow. And at the annual chili cook-off competition, none of the ladies would dream of sampling his chili or cornbread.

"Like many of you, I always enjoyed reading Warren's columns in *The Standard*," Rob said as he looked toward the back of the church and saw Holly rolling her eyes and mouthing, "*Oh please!*"

He shifted his gaze so that Holly was out of his sightline. The last thing he needed to do was giggle.

"His love of life revealed itself in everything he did, from his volunteer work to his careful preparation of some of the best gourmet dishes many of us have ever sampled."

Rob told of those times Warren would stop by the office with leftovers from a dinner he had served guests the night before. "Warren, always generously thinking of the rest of us at the paper, would call and say, 'Don't go out for lunch today, I want to bring you something wonderful.'"

In truth, Rob knew this was Warren's way of angling for extra space for his column or a more prominent byline, or perhaps the chance to confirm or deny some gossip he had heard while buzzing about town.

"In our grief," Rob said, concluding, "let us take time to be thankful for a life that enriched us as individuals and as a community. I'll always think of Warren preparing a gourmet dinner for the many people who loved him, and whom he loved in return. It is unlikely that any of us will meet someone as unique and as gifted as Warren Bradley again."

Thank God, Holly mouthed silently, adding an exaggerated sneer for Rob's benefit.

Rob wasn't sure if he had lived up to Alma's expectations. But after the service, each one of the Ladies of Liberty made it a point to go up and thank him for his "thoughtful and lovely words."

Even Bea, a woman who wore a dour expression every day of the year, walked over to Rob and said, "Thank you for being here for Warren. One of the very last times I spoke to him, he said, 'You have to take certain risks as a journalist if you're ever going to get the job done.' I'll always think of him when I see a man or a woman in your profession risking their safety so that the rest of us can live in a better world."

"Yes...right," Rob said, as he bit his lip to keep from smiling over the idea that Warren was anything like the daring, hardworking journalists that Bea had just described. It didn't surprise him that the comment had been taken out of context, or that it carried the apparent subtext: Warren's recent reporting on Grant Randolph's arrest had somehow led to his murder.

Rob then realized that Alma's ladies must be spreading this line of reasoning to anyone willing to listen. At the same time, he felt grateful for what he viewed as a momentary truce with his most persistent critics.

Rob was in mid-bite of a piece of chocolate cake when Holly tugged at his sleeve. "Jeez, you were spreading the manure a bit thick up there, don't you think?"

"Would you have preferred if I called him an officious little snob with an overinflated sense of self, who had a bad habit of airing other people's dirty laundry?" Rob said in a whisper.

"That would have been perfect!" Holly replied with a broad smile.

They both laughed. Holly then stood on her toes and whispered in Rob's ear, "I think Warren's killer is in this room! How about you?"

"That would be interesting," Rob said, as he returned the smile and nod of one more of the Ladies of Liberty.

Holly scanned the room. "So, let's see...how about Randolph's pal, Ray Sirica?"

"A little old, don't you think?"

"Yeah, but the guy works out like five days a week! He may be in his fifties, but he's built like a tree trunk. I don't think he'd have too much trouble carrying Warren around like a play doll and leaving him posed on his back deck."

Rob looked over at Sirica, who had come without Debbie to the service. While he never gave a man's physique a second thought, he could appreciate Holly's point. He had a benign smile, but there was a certain physical power about him that suggested he could have quickly suffocated Bradley if he was so inclined.

"And, of course, that letter he sent in about Warren spreading 'half-truths' regarding the incident between the Randolphs and saying, 'None of us would want to be placed in the crosshairs of the gossiping gourmet,'" Holly said, as she used air quotes. "I don't know him very well, but I wouldn't want to get up in that guy's grill."

In the middle of their exchange, Karin walked up. "What are you two up to? You look thick as thieves."

There was no jealousy in Karin regarding Rob and Holly's relationship. Readily aware that they'd been comrades under fire for several years, she jokingly referred to Holly as Rob's office wife.

In fact, Karin knew better than most the stress of Holly's job, having worked alongside Rob before leaving the paper to start a family.

"Believe me," she explained to any friend who asked, "Rob needs a strong woman to keep him in line, both at the paper and at home."

"We think there's a good chance that Warren Bradley's killer is in this room," Holly explained quietly.

"Really?" Karin said. "So, you're both going into the detective business as a sideline?"

"No, but we've bought into Eddie's theory that Warren knew his killer. We're thinking he might be here, hiding in plain sight," Rob explained.

At that moment, Eddie came over and joined them.

"See any suspicious looking characters?" Eddie asked Holly.

She gave a short laugh, "It's Sausalito, they all look pretty suspicious."

Chief Petersen cleared his throat as he walked up and stuck out his hand, "Rob, you did a good job up there."

"These occasions bring people together," Holly whispered into Karin's ear.

"Thanks," Rob said, as he thrust out his hand and shook Petersen's, who in turn greeted Eddie, Karin, and Holly.

Flanking Petersen were Chris Harding and Steve Hansen.

"He was a very nice man," Chris said, as he also shook hands with Rob and Eddie. After introductions, he nodded to Karin and Holly.

"We're still talking about that great caramel chicken he made for us a couple of weeks back," Hansen said. "Gosh, that was good. Not to mention some of his chocolate cherry brownies. I'm sure going to miss that guy!"

"Yeah, that man knew how to cook," Harding added with a broad smile. "That pasta with veal, sausage, and porcini ragu was also incredible!"

Rob was tempted to point out that the only thing he did better than cook was to spread rumors about his neighbors, but he kept that thought to himself.

"I suppose you're going to do a big piece about Warren and his death in next week's paper," Petersen said, causing Rob to wonder if he was fishing to see how he would approach the story.

Petersen, Rob assumed, was hoping that this would not turn into a "Sausalito Police dropped the ball once again" type of story. Or, in this particular case, dropped the body.

"You know, in a murder investigation, we're pretty much

sidelined. We don't have the staff or the resources to handle something like this," Petersen explained.

Hansen and Harding, who, like Petersen, were in dress blues, smiled and nodded in agreement with their chief.

"That's why we're thankful to get the assistance of Eddie here and the sheriff's department," Petersen added.

Eddie nodded and smiled, but did not comment.

After another round of handshakes, the three officers faded back into the crowd. Holly tugged Rob in close and whispered, "Hansen and Harding look healthy enough to throw Bradley over their shoulders and play dress-up with him as well."

"I suppose you think that Warren wouldn't cough up that caramel chicken recipe of his no matter how much they pressured him, so they murdered the old tattletale? You know Holly, you can't place everyone who is into bodybuilding on your suspect list. Go to that Gold's Gym up in Corte Madera that runs an ad for new members in our paper once a month, and you can arrest a couple dozen suspects on the spot."

"Who knows? Maybe if I tied Hansen and Harding up, I could slap the truth out of them."

"I think you've read one too many of those hot cop romance books you enjoy."

"A girl's got to have some fun," Holly pouted. "I don't know if you're aware of this, but the community news business can get a little dull at times."

"What? You mean you don't enjoy a good sewer replacement project cost overrun story now and then?" Rob raised his brows in mock horror. "Let's see what they have in this joint for dessert."

"Sadly, nothing that compares with Warren's chocolate cherry brownies," Holly warned.

L ater that afternoon, while the children were napping, Rob shared with Karin what he had learned from Eddie about Bradley's final "Heard About Town" column.

"They collected some of Warren's things and brought them to the county crime lab for analysis. They were happy to have his laptop. If it had named whom he dined with Tuesday night, they would have been a good deal happier. Unfortunately, that day's calendar just said, 'dinner here.' The most interesting item on it was his next 'Heard About Town' column, the one he never sent. In it, he demanded Randolph's resignation from the arts commission."

"Wow!" Karin said.

"Eddie is wondering if he was looking for a comment from Randolph about what he was planning to write. Maybe that's what brought Ray Sirica to his door sometime between six-thirty and seven that evening. His computer indicated that Warren made his final edits on that piece less than a half-hour earlier. But there was no mention in his column about his talking with Sirica or Randolph requesting a comment. Perhaps he intended to add that later but never got the opportunity."

"I'm sure Eddie would love to figure out what happened in the hours between when Bradley finished that column and when he wound up on the back porch with both his hands missing."

"From what I can tell, sweetheart, that's all Eddie's been thinking about for the last four days."

CHAPTER TWENTY

On Sunday morning, Rob awoke with the thought that he still needed a fresh angle on the Bradley murder investigation to lead his coverage for the upcoming edition of *The Sausalito Standard*.

The dailies, television, and radio outlets rushed in and covered the questions of who, how, when, where, and what. Now, it was Rob's turn to cover the story's most important aspect: the why.

To that end, Rob called Eddie to check on a couple of facts.

Eddie, always concerned about anything said over the phone, suggested that Rob come by his place. "On your way over, pick up some bagels," Eddie suggested. "You're looking for an angle, and I'm looking for some food. Seems like a fair trade."

Thirty minutes later, Sharon greeted Rob with a kiss on the cheek as he came through the door.

"There he is, the great orator himself!" Eddie announced.

"You should have heard him, Sharon! He had those old ladies weeping away for their dearly departed gossiping gourmet."

"Don't let him tease you, Rob. I ran into Marilyn Williams last night at Mollie Stone's Grocery. She said that all of the Ladies of Liberty were very impressed with your eulogy. She even let it slip that Alma saw you in a quote, 'new and more positive light.'"

"Oh, yes, our boy is quite the local star," Eddie said, putting on a cockney accent. "Sharon, put the kettle on so we can pour the lad a nice cuppa tea."

"Knock it off, you two. I've got to get serious and write a real piece for this week's paper. Hopefully, with some angle the pack of news hounds that blew through here last week never considered."

"So, your real purpose wasn't to bring us bagels but to pepper me with more questions?" Eddie scowled teasingly. "You want something the daily news boys and girls missed when they came racing through town last week? Well, fire away, Clark Kent. But remember, I haven't got much, pal."

"I'll leave you boys to your work," Sharon said, grabbing her hot cup of tea and a just-toasted buttered bagel. "But, Rob, think about giving Holly a shot at knocking out a lead on Warren Bradley. He once called her, and I quote, 'a woman of questionable morals.' Of course, he never said that to her face, nor in his column. Just a little gem he passed along to a neighbor who, in turn, passed it along to me."

"I'm just trying to get a little red meat to throw at my readers," Rob replied with a shrug.

"I know, darling," Sharon said, as she bent down and kissed Rob's cheek. "I'll leave you and Sherlock to your work."

"We both married interesting women," Eddie said, still in his pajamas, and putting his bare feet up on the chair Sharon had just left empty. "As for the Bradley case, it's pretty much where we left it Friday afternoon. Unless it's the murder of a VIP, investigators and the crime lab are off the hook when it comes to pushing cases forward over the weekend. But tell me what you're thinking, and let me see if I can add something to it."

"Some basic facts are already out on the table," Rob began, thinking out loud in the hope that an idea might occur to either of them. "Could I write about any suspects—that is, people questioned about their whereabouts at the time of the crime?"

"Okay, let's think about that," Eddie countered. "A lot of people in town know about the dust-up between Randolph and Bradley. You could ask me if Randolph has been questioned, given their contentious relationship, and I could say, 'The Randolphs flew to New York City on business Wednesday morning. They have been contacted by the Sausalito Police, who requested an interview upon their return.' I don't think that's been reported on and that should stir up some conversation."

"I'll use that for sure. What else?"

"You could also note that Warren had an elevated blood alcohol level at the time of his death. Police assume that he was entertaining a guest in the hours before he was killed and that no one yet has come forward to say that they were that guest or to suggest they know who that guest was."

"Can I mention that you interviewed Ray Sirica?"

"That's fine. The fact that Sirica was seen driving to Bradley's home in the hours before the Bradley murder originated with a neighbor. Just call the neighbor. You could also call Sirica for comment on the case."

"And if he doesn't disclose that the police interviewed him?" Rob asked.

"Just mention that Marin County Sheriff Department Detective Eddie Austin was seen entering his home, and he'll give that up. I didn't pull up in front of his house and walk up to his door shielded by a cloak of invisibility."

"True that," Rob laughed.

"Some of Sausalito's pinheads want to make Sirica out to be some mob syndicate guy, mostly because his last name ends in a vowel. That's small town nonsense! Sirica is about as hard to crack as a soft boiled egg," Eddie said with a shrug, as he took another bite of his bagel.

Rob nodded. "Okay, so what was Bradley's alcohol level? And what, if anything, did it mean?"

"It doesn't tell us much more than he had enough alcohol in him to get a DUI from Sausalito's finest, which isn't very much, as you and I learned as teenagers. But it was not at a level that would have contributed to his death. At least, not directly. The unknown factor is whether that amount of wine would make him sleepy enough that the apparent suffocation was much easier to perform. In that scenario, the alcohol would be a contributing factor. It's not an exact science; in a thirty-two-year-old, that scenario would be unlikely, but at seventy-plus, it could certainly have slowed his fight or flight response, if he ever responded at all.

"You could also say that minus his hands, we have no evidence of whether he scratched at his killer's arms, but as I told you before, any real struggle would have led to at least some bruising to the face, and there was none."

"So then, I can say that police suspect that Bradley's hands were severed, most likely as an attempt by the killer to send what, at this point, is an undetermined message or to eliminate incriminating evidence?"

"It's a free press, Rob. Say anything you want. Just do me the favor of passing by me any quotes you're attributing to me."

"Of course. And could it have been something more potent than wine that Bradley was drinking?"

"Interesting you should ask that. A simple blood test can't distinguish between beer, wine, and whiskey. But because the ME's staff wanted to check for any toxic substances slipped into Bradley's drink that would make killing him that much easier, they confirmed that the only identifiable element in the alcohol they found carried the chemical signature of wine."

"Could they still get accurate results, given that his body was not examined for approximately twenty-four hours after his death?"

"Yes, because he was outside on a mild Sausalito afternoon, and on a back porch that gets the sun only in the morning. That wouldn't affect decomposition of the body over a relatively short time period. More than likely, he was out there through most of the previous night, when temperatures were down in the upper forties. The afternoon high that following day briefly reached seventy degrees, but by that time of day Warren's back porch is already shaded, so it never got that hot. Now, on the other hand, leave a body on a porch swing in Houston for eighteen hours in the summertime, and you have a lot worse situation. In any significant heat, a body begins to decompose far more quickly."

"Did his stomach contents tell you much about the time he was killed?"

"Some. A good deal of what he ate that evening had not been fully digested, but it doesn't help us much as it pertains to a time frame. At the time a corpse is examined, a body's temperature can give you a reasonable guesstimate. But in a case like this, where you've got a dead guy sitting out on a porch on a chilly night and the following day, the old 'time of death' estimates can get a little squirrelly. Their best guesstimate is death occurred between eleven and midnight on Tuesday night."

"You must have done some things to look for prints and other biosignatures that the killer could have left behind."

"Listen to you, Rob—'biosignatures'! Well, la-dee-dah. You've been signing up for those FBI Citizen Academy forensic courses in your spare time, haven't you?" Eddie teased. "Granted, some of those Design Review Board meetings can get pretty heated, but they rarely lead to murder. Admit it—you don't mind the occasional murder mystery to spice things up in our quiet little town."

"Moving on," Rob muttered with a raised eyebrow and a half smile. "So, there's nothing you have in the way of prints, or physical evidence?"

"You're leading the witness," Eddie laughed while shaking his head. "The crime lab boys gave that place the once-over. The porch swing had prints, but they all belonged to the Sausalito PD and the fire guys, from when they were doing their Three Stooges act trying to move Warren off the swing and onto a stretcher. Other than that, we came up with a whole lot of nothing. I think our biggest break is that the body was found on the back porch of the cottage. Can you imagine the mess those cops and fire rescue boys would have made if they had gone traipsing through the house?"

"You still turned up a little helpful evidence inside, correct?"

"Yes, but it's a lot better to know that than to have to figure out where the contamination of the murder scene ends, and the evidence begins."

Eddie paused and took a long sip of tea. "Rob, personally, I have no doubt the killer was deranged. Not to suggest any killer is in his right mind. As we were saying the other day, Warren's killer was methodical enough to clean up his prints. He also knew to wait long enough after the victim died so that he could whack off the hands without making a mess. And he removed any napkins, paper, or cloth that could have contained his DNA. We went through the trash and Bradley's laundry bin and came away with nothing. Let's say he knows more than the average crime of passion killer about the condition of a dead body and how to avoid leaving DNA samples as evidence. I wouldn't want you sharing that particular information with our fellow citizens."

"I'll run by you whatever I'm thinking before I put it into print."

Eddie laughed. "If *The New York Times'* food critic gets in on this case, I doubt she or he will give me the same consideration."

"Not too likely that *The Times* will get involved. In fact, I think the San Francisco, Oakland, and Marin daily papers will drop the story until there is an arrest."

"That would be my guess. Dear Warren was only a star in our small corner of the world."

"I'll do a wrap-up story on the case this week. I'm sure I'll get some reactions from the ones most likely to want to give comments."

"I trust you have Alma on speed dial?"

Rob chuckled, "Heck yeah! The girl of my dreams."

"Go with the Randolph angle for now. You know— an undisclosed source close to the investigation suggested it was likely that Grant Randolph would be questioned upon his return from New York."

Rob nodded. "That will shake things up a bit."

"Whoa, wait a minute, Rob! I've got an even better angle. You should print the final column of the late great gossiping gourmet."

"What? ...*Why?*"

"A couple of reasons. First, it gives you something no one else has: a final plea from Warren Bradley to his fellow citizens to purge Randolph from his leadership position. Second, it will keep the Ladies of Liberty busy rounding up a lynch mob for Randolph. And third, if my guess is right and Bradley was killed by one of our fellow citizens whose initials are not GR, it encourages our killer to continue hiding in plain sight. Every day he or she thinks they're in the clear is one more opportunity to fall victim to your own conceit." Eddie grimaced. "Killing someone and thinking you've gotten away with it can be a real high. While Alma is busy campaigning for Randolph to be arrested, we might have the time we need to find Warren's real killer."

"Are you that sure Randolph isn't your man?"

"Absolutely!"

"Why?"

"Warren's killer waited around after the kill to clean up prints, chop off hands, and dress up the body. The whole crime was not only methodical; it was pretty damn cocky. If Randolph has an Achilles heel, it's his temper. This wasn't an act of uncontrollable rage. I'd be more suspect of Randolph if we found Bradley's body riddled with bullets, stabbed a dozen times, or beaten over the head with one of the great chef's iron skillets. I'm betting that whoever killed Bradley had been thinking about killing him for a very long time. This was meticulous, the opposite of rage."

By now, Rob was anxious to start writing his first full story on the Bradley killing—something that went far beyond the short posts he had written on the paper's website the past few days, all of which ended with a promise that there would be much more in the Wednesday print edition of *The Standard*.

"By the way, have you written anything about finding the body in the online version of your paper?" Eddie asked.

"No. I've been trying to keep myself out of it. Why?"

"For starters, there are a lot of cases where a killer is the first person to report the crime."

"Why the hell would *I* want to kill Warren Bradley?"

"I know you wouldn't. But in any normal investigation, your story would have been analyzed for discrepancies."

"What are you getting at?"

"It's simple, Rob. You should do a feature on finding Bradley. It tells the readers that, not only was he a contributor to the paper, but that you cared enough about him to want to learn why he vanished and missed the deadline for his weekly column. Particularly after he called to tell you he was in the process of completing it and promising you that it would get to you by your deadline. It ties you into the story in a personal way no other reporter, or news organization, can claim. It also is a great set-up for running Bradley's last column—those final words he promised to send you, but never had the chance to deliver."

"I have to admit, detective, you can be one smart newsman when you want to be."

"I love you too, pal. Now, get busy and make Miss Alma proud!"

CHAPTER TWENTY-ONE

Rob came home to an empty house. Karin had left a note, with her signature Hershey's Kiss sitting next to her Xs and Os, explaining that she'd taken their two children down to Dunphy Park to throw fishing lines out into Richardson Bay.

As always, it was unlikely that the children would catch anything with their kiddie rod-and-reel sets they had gotten for Christmas. Still, at ages five and three, it provided them with a two-hour diversion while Karin caught up on this week's copy of *People*.

There was no better time to tackle the first print article in what Rob suspected might be several stories on the Bradley case, particularly before an arrest was made and charges filed.

Rob was troubled by the fact that many homicides go unsolved. Approximately sixty-two percent of cases are cleared and thirty-eight percent go unsolved. Rob hoped Bradley's murder would not be one of those cases that stayed open. In a town where secrets have a remarkably short shelf life, he could not bring himself to believe that the name of Warren's killer would not surface in the days or weeks to come.

Surely, somewhere in town, someone knew something that would reveal critical clues. Small towns seem to work that way. Eventually, the whole story should begin to unravel and the killer exposed. It was a hope Rob clung to. Regardless of how engaged his readers were at this point, he knew their interest would diminish with each passing week.

As Rob began writing his story, he felt a bit of guilt over a sense of happiness that came over him. He wrote stories about chili cook-off contests and school science fairs. He could not help feeling excited as his fingers flew across his keyboard as a smile remained fixed on his face.

As Rob worked, he wondered if Warren might be alive today if he hadn't used his column as a bully pulpit. After all, his murder wasn't a case of being in the wrong place at the wrong time. Random, deranged killers don't knock on doors at the end of quiet streets and say, "It's been ages since I've suffocated someone and chopped off their hands. Mind if I come in and join you for dinner?"

Rob reasoned that any guilt he felt in publishing Warren's column was misplaced. The righteous vitriol Warren spewed in his recent columns regarding Randolph hadn't led to his murder. If it had, as Eddie pointed out, it's unlikely that Grant would have acted in such a methodical fashion. Warren's killer wasn't someone who had arrived after his dinner guest departed. It was far more likely that the killer was Warren's dinner guest.

Rob was not a betting man, but the more he thought about

this mystery, the more convinced he was that Eddie's line of reasoning made perfect sense.

When Monday's mail was pushed through the door slot, Holly raced out to retrieve them. "Five bucks says we're going to have a full mailbag column for our Sausalito edition this week."

"I'm not taking that bet," Rob shouted as Holly flew past him.

Already, a half-dozen letters had come in online, most of those tributes to the late chef. But, if Holly was right, the "blue hairs," as she often referred to the Ladies of Liberty, would send in their comments the old fashioned way: on light pink stationery decorated with flowers on top and bottom opposite corners of the page, with a matching envelope and a postage stamp promoting some worthy cause.

Holly sorted through the letters like a kid throwing packages around on Christmas morning.

"Oooh, here's one from Alma!" Holly said as she slipped a letter opener under the envelope's seal. "Ten bucks says she and her pals are already griping about the Sausalito PD not nabbing Warren's killer yet."

"I'm not betting against that either."

Holly quickly scanned Alma's missive, then exclaimed, "I knew this would be good!"

"Okay, give it over. What does Sausalito's grand dame have to say from her lofty perch?"

Holly's eyes quickly scanned the second of two pages, handwritten on rose-colored stationery in perfect penmanship in deep blue ink that contrasted dramatically against the sheet. "Ha," Holly declared, as she slapped down the pages on the corner of Rob's desk and said, "Here, read it yourself! I think you've got a new admirer."

"Oh, great. Now what?" Rob asked. As he grabbed the pages off the edge of his desk, Holly gave a sinister giggle.

It started as he expected, with Alma recalling the "artistry of Warren's cooking...the charm and wit of his disarming humor, his kindness and generosity, and what will be most missed, his tireless service on behalf of our community."

She then added, "The Sausalito police have been longtime recipients of Mr. Bradley's unstinting generosity, in the preparation and presentation of a monthly gourmet luncheon for our brave men and women in blue. I trust that they will honor his kindness by being vigilant and unstinting in their efforts to bring this vicious killer to justice."

"Wow!" Rob looked up at Holly, who winked knowingly at him. "You're right; she laid it on pretty thick."

"Oh, you haven't come to the best part. Keep reading."

He quickly scanned through a few more lines about Warren's Easter ham dinner at the senior center and his gourmet cookie packages, which were distributed during the holidays each year to a long list of neighbors and friends.

But then, Rob came to his name and started to read the letter aloud.

"I guess you mean this part: 'As a small community, we have only *The Sausalito Standard* to speak on behalf of justice—a single voice that must remain vigilant in pursuit of the truth. I have not always been of like mind with the editorial policy of our local newspaper—for example, when it urges modernization, while others, like I, have called for restraint. But, as its publisher, Rob Timmons, demonstrated during his moving tribute to his distinguished longtime columnist, this is a time when all Sausalitans must stand together and insist that every resource needed be applied in pursuit of this crazed killer, even if it leads to shocking revelations involving people in high places. Now is the time when every rock must be lifted to see what evil lurks beneath.'"

"I imagine the 'people in high places' means her least favorite member of the arts commission," Rob murmured. "You're right, Holly! The old girl went all out with this one." He looked down and read Alma's closing lines, "I trust that Mr. Timmons will be a tireless voice in following the trail wherever it leads. Now is the time for answers!"

"Sounds like you and Alma are becoming an item."

Rob shrugged and causally said, "The old girl looks particularly fetching out on the bay at sunset."

"You mean when anchored to a block of cement?"

"Oh, Holly, you're such a romantic." Rob rolled his eyes. "Okay, let's cut the nonsense. We've got a week's worth of papers to get out. And, by the way, on page fifteen, I've decided to run Warren's final 'Heard About Town' column."

"What?" Holly squawked. "You're going to stir up a lot of trouble if you run that! It will be like a voice from the grave. And any chance you and Karin had of being invited to the Randolphs for cocktails will go right out the window for good."

"Frankly, I see it as a final tribute to Warren." Rob was determined not to tell Holly the truth—that Eddie asked for him to use Warren's final column as a distraction to focus more heat on Randolph, hopefully putting the real killer at ease.

"Shame on you, Rob. I get it—great for business and all that. But it sure will make Randolph's life miserable."

Rob winced. He knew she was right.

At the same time, if Eddie was right, and the tactic helped to flush out the killer, in the long run he'd be doing Randolph a great favor.

"If I were you, I'd watch my back. If Randolph did kill Warren, my guess is that you're numero uno to be victim numero dos."

n Wednesday, *The Sausalito Standard* carried an unusual banner headline:

Who Murdered Warren Bradley?

Rob knew he was milking the murder for all he could, but if he was ever going to have an issue that would be read by everyone in town, this was likely to be the one. Barring, of course, the interest over a suspect being apprehended.

Knowing he needed to follow through on the goal he set for himself of having information that no other news outlet carried, he contacted both Warren's neighbor and Ray Sirica for comments.

Ray couldn't keep the anxiety out of his voice. His wish from the moment he learned of Warren's murder was that he had not gone up to see Bradley at his home hours before his murder.

While Ray tortured himself, Debbie reminded him, "You didn't have a crystal ball. No one would have guessed what was about to happen. It was just a case of bad timing. Leave it at that."

Of course, Ray already knew this. "Believe me," he told her, "I wish I could turn back the clock on that decision."

Naturally, there was a part of both Debbie and Ray that wished they had never eaten at the same café in Healdsburg on the day Grant and Barbara walked in and sat down beside them. It was simply one more example of bad timing.

Despite his frustration, Ray was forthcoming when Rob called for a comment about his meeting with Bradley on that fateful night. "I thought the situation was escalating between Grant and Warren," he explained. "Those columns put a lovely couple in a terrible light all because they had a colossal misunderstanding. I don't mind you quoting me saying that I think Warren was unfair and unkind to both of them. I went up there to explain to Bradley that their entire fight, serious as it had been, in reality was nothing more than a comedy of errors. But Warren wasn't interested in writing a story about how one misunderstanding can lead to another and lead to awful consequences. In fact, he told me that he had a guest arriving shortly. And then he added, in these exact words, 'Please leave now.'"

Rob knew Ray had to be uncomfortable discussing Grant's situation with the publisher of a community newspaper that played a role in making his friends' lives difficult. Rob regretted that, along with the inevitable balancing act he faced every week attempting to remain neutral in Sausalito's ongoing social and political infighting, the platform he gave Warren might have played a role in his murder.

He looked for the words to explain to Ray that he and Warren were two very different people. "Warren's gossip column has upset people in the past," Rob explained. "As you know, this is a small town. When some of the lifers around here decide you're not their sort of people, not only will they imagine that you had a part in Bradley's killing, they also presume you committed every murder in a hundred-mile radius."

❦

"**D**on't you think you went a little hard on Grant Randolph?"

Karin's question had Rob choking on his lunch. The latest issue of *The Standard* had just been delivered to their home mailbox.

"How so?" he asked reluctantly, not sure he wanted to hear her answer.

"Well...you go into the run-in he had with Warren at the opera park event."

He shrugged. "And?"

"I don't know...It's just that it puts Randolph in such a bad light! Frankly, I feel sorry for the guy."

"I agree with you. But it's a part of the story. If days before some guy gets killed, a third of the people in town see you having a confrontation with the victim who's found murdered and dismembered, it's not going to put you in a good light. And it's probably nothing more than rotten timing that the Randolphs left for New York only twelve hours after Bradley's body was discovered. But those are the facts, and you can't objectively edit them out of the story. Remember that in the news business you can get in trouble for what you choose to leave in or leave out of a story."

Noting Karin's silence, Rob again jumped into the void. "When you're the publisher and lead reporter for a small town newspaper, you're swimming in a fishbowl. That's one of the things I most like about doing the other editions, in Tiburon/Belvedere, Mill Valley, and Ross Valley; I don't know near as many people that I pass than when I'm in Sausalito. Both of us grew up here. We're the third generation of the Timmons family to live in this house, and *The Standard* has been published in town since the nineteen-fifties."

"...And, so?" Karin asked.

"More so than any other town in Marin, what I do here is looked at under a microscope. I guarantee you: for every one person who asks me why I mentioned Grant Randolph in the Bradley story, there's another nine who would wonder why I did not mention their confrontation."

"You're right, Rob. I can see that. But then running that last column of Bradley's, isn't that rubbing salt in the wound?"

"Just between us, that was Eddie's contribution to this week's edition."

"You don't mean he wrote it, do you?"

"No, of course not. It's Bradley's actual last column. But Eddie knew it would stir up more suspicion about Randolph. He believes that Bradley's killer lives or works, or both, right here in Sausalito. The more attention that's focused on

Randolph, the greater the possibility that the real killer will let down his guard—in other words, hopefully, get careless."

"No one but you and Eddie knows this?"

"I haven't even mentioned it to Holly. She too thought I'd lost my marbles when I told her I was running Bradley's final column."

"I can't imagine what the Randolphs are going to think when they see this coverage, not to mention the column. Bradley went over the top with that bit about 'expelling this viper from our midst.'"

"Like his mentor, Alma Samuels, Warren had a flair for the dramatic. Personally, I think Randolph is probably a decent guy. But he's certainly got a bad temper. Perhaps he should cut back on all that weightlifting—maybe he's dealing with a little too much testosterone. That said, going from having some anger issues to doing what was done to Bradley is a pretty big leap. But if God forbid, Grant Randolph did kill Warren Bradley, and I never mentioned that night at the opera incident, I'd be laughed out of town."

She shrugged. "You're probably right about that as well."

"I never told you this, but when I was delivering the Bradley eulogy, I was convinced that his killer was standing there in the church, watching me and listening to everything I said. And as you know, Commissioner Randolph was thousands of miles away."

"That old church doesn't hold many people—probably less than two hundred. It would be pretty creepy if the killer were sitting there looking at you." Karin shuddered at the thought, then stood up. "I've got to walk down to Sparrow Creek to pick up the children." She walked over and kissed Rob on the cheek. "Even if the Randolphs had stayed in town this past week and Warren had not been murdered, I have a feeling they wouldn't have gone to another outdoor opera event."

"Perhaps it's a good thing Randolph got out of town when he did; that old church has high rafters. Alma herself would have provided the rope if she thought she could get away with some old-fashioned frontier justice."

"That's my point. In a town this small, one bad misstep, and you're guilty in the court of public opinion." Karin sighed and shook her head in disappointment. "I wouldn't be surprised if, make that when, this whole thing blows over, those poor people move back to New York. I guess they're learning first-hand the downside of living in a town where everyone knows your name."

CHAPTER TWENTY-TWO

When Rob returned to the office after lunch Holly announced, "Your girlfriend, Alma, called. She hopes you have a moment to call her back." Holly pursed her lips and made a kissing sound.

"Hey, give the old lady a break. I don't have any problem with Alma wanting to know who killed her favorite chef."

"Gosh, you're a little touchy today!" Holly frowned as she headed back to her office.

Rob felt terrible, knowing that he was taking some of his frustration out on his office mate. He was keenly aware that his readers were all waiting for answers. But if the cops didn't have any, more specifically, Eddie, what in the world did Warren's loyal fan base think he had?

Nonetheless, Rob quickly called Alma, aware that this new détente between them could expand readership, resulting in increased advertising revenue—something he would happily welcome.

Alma picked up on the first ring. Her tone was unusually pleasant. "I loved this week's edition of *The Standard*," she purred.

At the top of the final "Heard About Town" column, Rob placed a brief statement: "Written by Warren Bradley, just hours before his death. This document was uncovered by law enforcement officials working on his homicide, and was made available to readers of *The Standard*."

"It's extraordinary," Alma continued, "that he wrote about this dangerous man, Randolph, hours before his murder. If Warren were alive today his first question would be: Why is Grant Randolph not in custody?"

Rob was sure this was Alma's opening salvo in her hope of organizing a lynch mob.

Cautiously, he said, "I heard that the Randolphs left for New York City early on the morning after Warren's body was found."

"I had heard that, too, and I'm sure it sounds highly suspicious to you as well."

"If not suspicious, rotten timing at a minimum."

Both paused, realizing they might be on a path to expressing divergent points of view.

"In any event, I was hoping that in your next edition you will keep a bright light shining on Grant Randolph's whereabouts," Alma said. "It wouldn't surprise me in the least if they both decided to extend their visit to New York. What thoroughly distasteful people!"

There were a few moments of awkward silence; Rob gazed out his window at passing tourists walking into the shops of Princess Court as he considered his response. "Randolph is certainly at the top of everyone's suspect list. At the same time, it's hard to second-guess where the investigation stands at any given moment," Rob suggested. "The police are staying pretty quiet and that's not making my job any easier."

"Well, sail on, brave soul. I just wanted to be sure you're pursuing Warren's killer without hesitation. I feel quite certain you're doing exactly that. In fact, every member of the Ladies of Liberty is at this very moment singing your praises."

Talk about offering up a carrot as opposed to Alma's usual stick.

As Rob thanked her and hung up, he turned his swivel chair away from the window to the faded blue couch that sat on the wall opposite his desk. Holly sat there, staring at him with a mischievous smile. She arched a brow. "So, what did the queen of darkness have to say for herself?"

"Sheesh! I haven't seen you this excited since Paul Simon stopped his car on Princess Street to ask you for directions."

Holly waved away Rob's jibe with a swish of her wrist. "If the least likely suspect is the killer—which is what happens all the time in murder mysteries—then I'm guessing Alma did it."

"If she killed Bradley, she must have hired one of the counter boys at Venice Gourmet as an accomplice. She certainly wasn't the one preparing the wrist chops or tossing Warren's body around like an antique Ken doll."

"That might be it! She's the dinner guest—no surprise there. She gets him good and soused. Then, she lets Benedetto —who can handle a cleaver on those old hard salamis like they're butter—step in and finish the job."

"Alright Agatha, let's get back to work. *The Peninsula Standard* is three hours from final deadline."

As Holly re-checked the completed layout pages for the Tiburon/Belvedere edition, she cheered herself by imagining Alma Samuels working in the laundry at a California state prison for the remaining years of her life.

🐚

One week earlier, the day Warren's murder was a top Bay Area news story, the Siricas made an urgent call to Grant and Barbara.

"Are you sitting down?" Ray asked. "In fact, put your cell on speaker. Barbara has to hear this as well!"

Grant did as Ray suggested and motioned Barbara over.

"Hi, Ray. Hi, Debbie. What's up?" Barbara asked.

Debbie couldn't contain herself. "Warren Bradley was murdered last night!"

"What?" Barbara and Grant shrieked in unison.

"You've got to be kidding," Barbara murmured.

"This is no joke," Ray responded. "I'm reading about it right now, on the *San Francisco Chronicle*'s website. I'll forward you the article as soon as we get off this call. Grant, I hate to say this, but it may not look so great for you, considering it happened just hours before you left town. Not to mention the blowout you had with Warren at the opera event."

Grant was silent for a moment. Finally, he declared, "Ray, Debbie, hand to God, I had absolutely nothing to do with this."

"We would never suspect you of killing that old troll," Ray assured him.

"We love you both. I'm sure, before long, they'll find whoever did this," Debbie added.

For a brief moment, after their call ended, Grant and Barbara were lost in their thoughts. But when they caught each other's eyes, Barbara noticed the upturned corners of Grant's lips. Soon, her smile matched his. "I think this calls for drinks," Grant declared. "What do you say we go to the bar over at the Waverly?"

Barbara laughed. "I'll drink to that."

When they arrived and settled in, their first toast was to Warren's memory. "I know it's sad," Barbara said, "but he was a mean-spirited little louse! I couldn't believe what he wrote about me. I'm trying to get a little publicity for myself about working a new job at a prestigious gallery, and he makes it sound like I thought the women in the league were a bunch of silly fools!"

"He was a gasbag," Grant said. "I'm not going to let myself feel sorry for him. Based on the experience we had with him, I would think the number of possible suspects the police are looking into could fill a jumbo jet."

A week later, when Ray and Debbie read them excerpts from Warren's final column, the beleaguered couple knew this was not the time to fly back to the Bay Area. Based on their itineraries, they had already decided to extend their stay in New York. Now, they thought it wise to continue their stay indefinitely. Being two more anonymous faces in a sea of humanity was an unexpected comfort.

I t was apparent from the number of readers' letters arguing for Randolph's arrest that Alma and her Ladies of Liberty had instigated a letter-writing campaign.

On Thursday afternoon, Eddie called to say that the Randolphs had extended their stay in New York City another week.

Eddie had not been able to make their usual Friday afternoon date at Smitty's, but on Saturday, he pulled up outside of Rob's home in his unmarked county sheriff's car. Kissing Karin on the cheek, he asked, "Do you mind if I borrow your husband for a couple of hours?"

"Fine with me. I was about to take the kids up to Cloudview Park. One of the Sparrow Creek kids, little Anna, is having her third birthday party up there." Karin pointed toward Rob's home office and said, "Get him out of the house. He needs some fresh air. He's been spending way too much time in there."

Eddie found Rob at his desk lost in thought. With less than seventy-two hours before the next deadline for his Sausalito edition, he was feeling discouraged. His attempts to spin another Bradley story out of what little new information he had was harder than he had imagined.

He was happy to accept Eddie's invitation to go for a drive. Yes, a change of scenery would do him good. And, perhaps, he might get lucky and hear something that he could use to satisfy his readers' hunger for more revelations in a mystery that was still the talk of the town.

The two friends drove to Mill Valley and went up a back road that climbed one of the flanks of Mount Tamalpais, which rises twenty-eight hundred feet and dominates the surrounding landscape.

Eddie pulled off onto a dirt road and parked at a trailhead known mostly to locals. As Eddie had hoped, there were no other cars around. "Come on, let's go for a little walk."

Rob smiled and nodded approvingly. "We haven't been to this spot since we were in high school."

They walked along a trail that hugged the hillside. It offered great views but had a steep drop that was far too narrow for casual hikers. After going a half-mile down the path, they came to a dugout where a boulder had come to rest, perhaps centuries earlier. The rock was a perfect example of a bench placed by God for a select few to stop and enjoy the view.

They pulled themselves up and sat down on the massive stone, which was warmed by the midday sun. As they looked out at a vista that included tree-covered hillsides and distant views of the Pacific, Rob said in a low voice, "Remember when we used to come up here with Trevor and Alex to smoke pot?"

Eddie inhaled the fresh mountain air. "We were certainly young and dumb. Pot, beer, and steep drop-offs are probably not the safest combination."

"And let's not forget the occasional mountain lion out for a stroll with her young cubs," Rob laughed.

"It's amazing to think how many things we did as kids that we would never want our kids to do."

"Amen to that, pal."

They watched in silence as two hawks circled the steep canyon looking for prey far below. Finally, Eddie said, "I need your help. What I'm about to tell you can't go any further than the two of us."

"Is it about the Bradley killing?"

"Bingo."

"Whatever it is, Eddie, we've been like brothers most of our lives. Just tell me, and I'll put into print only what you think will help to solve your case and certainly nothing that would hinder your investigation."

Eddie's smiled as he patted Rob on the shoulder. "I know that. Let me start by telling you that Grant Randolph had nothing to do with the murder of Warren Bradley."

"You sound pretty sure about that."

"I've been close to the guys in the ME's office for a long time. They can be your best friends in a murder investigation. When they know something, small or big, they get a hold of me right away."

"Yeah...and..."

"It's about 99 percent certain that Bradley's killer was left-handed."

Rob gave a low whistle. "How did they figure that out?"

"The angle at which that meat cleaver smashed through Bradley's wrists gave it away. Even on a dead man, it takes a reasonable amount of force to cut through all those bones and tendons. It's highly unlikely that our killer is right-handed but used his left hand to cut off Warren's hands."

Rob shook his head. "How does the county's medical examiner get to keep a gem like that quiet?"

"Simple. This is an ongoing murder investigation. In pursuit of the victim's killer, you're not serving the cause of justice to turn over every card you're holding to the public. If you all but eliminate right-handed individuals, approximately 90 percent of the entire population, and you consider the upper body strength of our killer and our relative certainty that Warren knew his killer, as over nine out of ten victims do, the pool of suspects drops to a much smaller number."

"Do the nitwits at the Sausalito Police Department know about this?"

"Nope. There's no real need to let them know. They don't have an investigator working the case, so sharing that kind of information with them increases the chance of it getting out into the general public."

"I agree. Now for my sixty-four thousand dollar question: where do I come in? In other words, how can I help? And how is it that you know Randolph is right-handed?"

"Let me answer your second question first. We went through the files of some previous art commission meetings. The powers at city hall, in league with Alma and her gang, are hoping that we're closing in on Randolph. They were only too happy to help. There is a slew of photos of the commission at work...several of which show Randolph holding a pen in his right hand as he's taking notes during a meeting. As for the other part of your question, you're a damn good investigator Rob, whether you realize it or not, and I'm going to need an extra set of hands—no puns, please—to cover possible suspects and motives."

"How many are there?"

"Bradley fed on the minutiae of life in Sausalito. I suspect he either knew too much or said too much about one of his neighbors. Two-thirds of the town is looking for his or her favorite suspect, which, as we discussed, is fine with me. The more people convinced that Randolph is the killer the better off we are. We don't want to do anything to spook the real killer into pulling a disappearing act."

"Given the strength the killer needed, I don't suppose there's any chance that the killer is a female?" Rob asked.

"Not unless the killer is a left-handed female bodybuilder. I don't know any women in Sausalito that fit that description. Do you? The longer the townies keep their focus on Randolph, the better I like it."

"So, what do you want me to do?"

"I need you to be my go-to guy for in-depth information on our victim. The more we can learn about Bradley's life, the closer we might get to identifying his killer. Right now, you're on good terms with Alma and her gang of busybodies. Tell them you're planning a retrospective on the life and times of Warren Bradley. Once you start digging into his past, hopefully some actionable information will fall into place. There are only a handful of people like Karin, you, and me, who grew up in Sausalito, living their whole lives in that tiny fishbowl. The vast majority of people in most Marin communities arrived ten, twenty, or thirty years ago. Bradley came to Sausalito approximately twenty-five years ago. Bottom line, Rob, we need to know more about Bradley's life before he showed up in town."

"I'm fine with all this, if you think I can help," Rob assured Eddie. "You're right that there are a lot of people in town who would string up Randolph and be done with it."

"Fortunately for Randolph, he might appear to be the obvious killer, but this isn't the Wild West anymore."

Rob chuckled. "That's a good thing for me as well. Nosy, pushy journalists, asking too many questions, didn't have a long life expectancy in the early years of California."

"Speaking of nosy, how long did Warren write his column for *The Standard?*"

"About six years."

"Can you take the time to go back and give those old columns a closer look? I'm sure Randolph isn't the only one who would have liked to murder that infamous busybody. We'll probably follow a lot of leads that go nowhere, but hopefully, we can pull one thread that causes this whole thing to unravel."

"But what about those missing hands, Eddie? What the hell was that about?"

"Trust me, pal. When we find the killer, the mystery of the missing hands will fall into place."

CHAPTER TWENTY-THREE

R
ob was excited about Eddie's request. He was right to ask that everything, at least for now, be kept between the two of them.

"If there are any leaks, it could spoil our efforts and put us back at square one," Eddie reminded him. "We have to keep this from everyone: even, Karin, Sharon, and that super sleuth assistant of yours, Holly."

While it was true that most of Rob's work would bore a crime reporter to distraction, he wasn't a complete stranger to the persistent and patient work of investigative reporting. He had uncovered several cases of bribery and misappropriation of funds in city and county agencies. Two recent examples: a Tiburon council member taking kickbacks in exchange for his vote; and a Mill Valley council member provided with the use of a Lake Tahoe vacation home by a local architect whose projects she consistently voted to support.

Rob began his task by explaining to Holly that he was doing

a retrospective on Warren. "Please e-mail me his entire file of columns."

"Are you sure, Rob?" Holly asked in surprise. "That's a lot of garbage to search through!"

"Don't worry. I haven't lost my mind. I want to scan through Bradley's work and get a better feel for what he wrote."

"Okay, boss. It's your call."

During his spare time in the evenings, and over the next few workdays, Rob reviewed all of Warren's two hundred and ninety-six "Heard About Town" columns. Once again, it stirred Rob's regrets as to why he had published Warren's column for so long. He realized, however, that it had been a marriage of convenience, similar to arrangements he had made with other retired seniors in his small corps of community reporters. Fortunately, his other writers did not have Warren's love of gossip, or the desire to settle personal scores with a variety of fellow citizens.

Warren, however, took cattiness to extremes, which might have been a reflection of the uniquely sharp elbows found in Sausalito's political and social scene.

Most of Warren's items and columns dealt with his musings about "modern day life," or his mentions of special birthdays. In this regard, he never missed those of Alma Samuels, Bea Snyder, Ethel Landau, Robin Mitchell, or other "Ladies of Liberty Superstars." He faithfully provided reporting of various Sausalito Women's League events— notably the annual holiday follies—and coverage of the endless game of musical chairs for seats on the town's commissions, committees, and the grand prizes: the city council, planning commission, and design review board. All of it was grist for Bradley's gossip mill.

Now and then, Warren unsheathed the cutting edge of his words, turning his column into a weapon as opposed to a platform for idle chatter.

In the column's second year, he aimed his fire at a recently elected member of the city council, Robert Allan, who, in a nasty encounter with one of his disappointed supporters, suddenly slapped her in the midst of a heated exchange. Allan called it nothing more than "an admonishing tap to her cheek." The one on the receiving end of what Warren called "the slap heard round the world" called it a "hideous and unprovoked act of violence." Subsequent columns made it apparent that Warren's mailbag was overwhelmed with demands for the young Mr. Allan to resign. The gentleman did just that, and soon after moved out of town. His departure caused Warren, in his typically snide fashion, to wonder aloud "if Mr. Allan will be missed?"

It seemed unlikely that Allan returned to Sausalito to murder Warren, but he was indeed a name to be added to Eddie's list.

The following year, in an event far less public than the infamous "slap heard round the world," Warren implied that Carrie Kahn was pocketing a portion of the raffle money raised for the purchase of new fitness equipment for "our brave men and women of the Sausalito Fire Department." In his usual style, he stopped just short of making an accusation and used the comments and concerns of others to build his case—often without attribution. He wrote, for example, "sources, who wish to remain anonymous, have told this columnist that…"

At first, Kahn and a few of her friends complained loudly in letters to the editor. But, as she later explained, she chose "not to pursue legal remedies for the wrongs committed by Mr. Bradley," whom she went on to refer to as "a mean-spirited little man."

Her decision not to pursue Bradley could have been for several reasons, but the two most likely were she had pocketed some of the raffle money, or she did a lousy job of keeping all her ticket stubs alongside final running totals. Having realized that in a libel suit, it is the burden of the accused to provide evidence that there was no basis for the stated claims, she was left with no logical choice but to live under the cloud that now hung over her. For that reason, Rob nominated Carrie to Eddie's list of suspects in spite of Eddie's belief that only a male killer could have had the brute force to chop through Warren's wrists so cleanly and, more significantly, move Bradley's body onto that swing.

Of course, there were others, all of whom Rob concluded were likely suggested for Warren's court of public opinion by his patroness, Alma, and her lieutenants.

When Rob finished reading all the columns, he mumbled to himself, "If Warren Bradley were alive today, I'd dump him *and* his column!"

If he had put an end to Warren's column a year or more ago, would Bradley be alive today? Perhaps some people who acted carelessly or impetuously would not have suffered Warren's public form of humiliation. But what was done was done. Rob knew there was little value in crying over spilled ink. To run a small newspaper in one or more small towns comes with its share of regrettable moments. This was one more regret that Rob needed to put behind him.

Having picked up little that might have driven one of the

injured targets of Warren's past columns to go as far as murder, it was time to move on to the next step: Who was Warren Bradley before he arrived in Sausalito?

W hen Rob called Alma and explained he'd like to interview her for a Warren Bradley retrospective, she was delighted. Without hesitation, she suggested that Rob join her for tea at four that afternoon.

Rob was undoubtedly familiar with the Samuels' mansion and the lovely piece of property on which it stood. Nevertheless, when Louise showed him into the home's sunroom, he was impressed with his surroundings.

Alma entered and reached out to take his hand. She immediately said, "Mr. Timmons, I'm delighted to welcome you to my home."

"Call me Rob, please."

"Of course—Rob," she said with a faint smile. "Let me start by saying how pleased I am that you are doing a piece on dear Warren's life. His death is an unspeakable tragedy, and he should never be forgotten! He was too kind, and too vigilant a journalist to be forgotten. The Ladies of Liberty have been discussing where we might erect a statue in Warren's memory. Perhaps, a bust sitting atop a pillar in the plaza outside of city hall would be the best choice. There are many groups, charities, and organizations that I'm certain would contribute to the project."

Rob felt a shiver go down his spine over the thought of a Warren Bradley memorial, particularly after completing his review of Warren's columns. Perhaps a third of the town would like a bronze bust on a marble pillar, a third would agree to a likeness of Warren's head placed on a spike, and the final third would remain undecided as they were on nearly every local issue.

Alma thanked Louise, who placed a tray of tea and cookies on the antique coffee table between them. "Now, Rob, fire away. I hope you're doing a thorough job in making Warren come alive again for everyone who knew him."

"I hope so, as well. Let me begin by asking if you remember when you first met Warren."

"Confident you'd ask, I was thinking about that this morning. My best guess is twenty-five years ago—or perhaps a little more."

Rob nodded. "That would have been close to the time Warren settled in Sausalito. I'm also uncertain as to where he lived before he arrived here. Did he ever share that information with you?"

Alma frowned. "Warren and I discussed many things over the years, but I don't recall the topic of his years before Sausalito coming up. He did mention that he studied at the Culinary Institute, in Saint Helena. He also said that he majored in finance, at Carnegie Mellon in Pittsburgh. But I don't have any idea of the actual years he attended either of those distinguished institutions."

"I understand that Warren was over seventy at the time of his death."

She nodded. "That seems about right."

"I reread all his columns to see if he mentioned his childhood, or his life before Sausalito. Unfortunately, he never did.

My guess, however, is that he grew up back east. Did he ever discuss with you where that was?"

"I'm sorry, Rob, not that I recall. I guess there is very little I know about Warren's life before Sausalito." Her eyes opened wider at this realization. "It's always been said that he was in the world of banking, or finance. But I cannot recall our ever discussing that time of his life."

Trying to put a smile on his face to cover his disappointment, Rob shifted his focus to Bradley's more recent years.

But when they got to the topic of Warren's columns, Alma became agitated. "Warren sat in the very chair you're sitting in now when I told him that I was concerned for his safety. Just one look at that Grant Randolph and you could tell he was a brute! But Warren was simply fearless. He was, by his very nature, a truth teller."

Realizing that the conversation had devolved into a series of endless stories about Bradley's "extraordinary generosity" and his "remarkable culinary skills," Rob thanked Alma for her hospitality. But before he could make a hasty retreat, Alma took his hand in both of her hands. Staring intently up at the smile he had fixed on his face, she declared, "Whoever wanted to harm dear Warren may want to harm you as well. But, unlike Warren, you have a wife and two children, so please be careful, Rob! I can't imagine what the loss of a second great journalist would mean to our small town."

As Rob backed out of the driveway, he wasn't sure whether to take Alma's performance of tea and sympathy as kindness or gamesmanship. What he did know was that he had no more actionable information regarding Warren's past than he had when Eddie asked him to dig something up on his background.

But, as every investigative reporter knows, you have to set

aside frustrations over one or more blind alleys and keep pushing forward.

On the short winding drive through Sausalito's labyrinth of steep hills leading down to his office, which was located steps away from the edge of the bay, Rob thought about his next move. At least one benefit, however, came out of his meeting: he suspected that, on some level, Alma too was uneasy with the thought that her beloved Warren entered her close circle of friends without a known past.

From phone interviews with Ethel Landau, Bea Snyder, Robin Mitchell, and Marilyn Williams, Rob came away with nothing more than the sparse facts Alma Samuels had already shared.

He endured the pain of their endless stories concerning Warren's "noble efforts and volunteering spirit" in bringing food for one event or another, and offering help in any way he could with those causes that were most important to the Ladies of Liberty.

But Warren Bradley's life before Sausalito remained a mystery.

Eddie worked a late shift on Friday. Once again, he bowed out of the end-of-week meet-up at Smitty's with Rob and Holly.

Still, before leaving the office, Rob asked Holly if she wanted to join him for a drink. They had both worked a long week, and Rob's increasing frustration with Bradley's empty past led to his being short with her for most of the week.

"Is this your way of saying you want to kiss and make up?"

Holly teased. "If it is, then yes, I'll allow you to buy back my affections with a martini."

"Good! I was hoping you'd say yes, so grab your bag and let's get out of here."

Ten minutes later, after they settled in on the quiet far end of Sausalito's most popular downtown watering hole, the No Name Bar, Rob took a long pull on a bottle of Guinness while Holly took a much-needed sip of her beloved martini.

"So, what's up, boss? You've been more than your usual grumpy self this week."

"I'm sorry about that. I told you I've been trying to put together a piece about Warren Bradley's life, and—"

"Are you sure you want to do that?" She frowned.

"I have to! His murder is the biggest news story we've had around here in a long time, and for six years he wrote a column for the newspaper. Sausalito readers expect me to do a complete piece on his life," Rob explained, using the same line he'd used with each member of the Ladies of Liberty.

"Okay, so what's the problem?"

"I keep running into the same blank wall! No one knows anything about Warren before he showed up in Sausalito. Nothing other than the couple of stories, attending Carnegie Mellon in Pittsburgh, and later the Culinary Institute of America up in Napa, that I think he seeded. Neither school has any record of him attending. Even in the career he supposedly retired from—a position in finance—I can't find any link to him holding any position in that field. It's like the guy one day just popped up out of the ground."

"Gosh! I guess he was even creepier than I imagined."

"Alma and her entire gang all spin the same story, but by now I'm pretty certain it's all fiction."

"Fiction that Warren must have created."

"So, Holly, I was thinking—"

"Say no more, boss. I'll see what I can do to the track the guy down—hopefully, get us some idea of where he came from, and what he was doing before he landed here and started delighting some people and irritating others."

"That would be great. I don't think there's anything sinister to all this, but his past seems to have been buried, and I'd love to know why."

"Happy to do it. Maybe I'll get lucky and turn up something nasty on the old busybody. I'd love that, after all the misery he stirred up for others."

"Boy, you seriously did not like Bradley."

"In addition to his not-to-subtle suggestions that I was a libertine woman—based on the fact that I'm mid, uh, early thirties and single—there's the whole thing with Carrie Kahn and the supposed raffle money embezzlement nonsense. Carrie's a bit dippy; I do not doubt that. But so are half the people in this town. I don't think she did a great job of sepa-rating the cash she got from tips working behind the bar at Bob and Herb's from all the tickets she was selling to customers. Still, that jerk's innuendoes just tore her up! She thought the real reason Warren humiliated her is she didn't come rushing over every time his wine glass needed refilling. I know it's not a big deal, Rob, but I'm telling you: the guy was a sneaky, creepy, SOB."

"I only wish I'd been paying more attention to what he was writing each week. I probably would have put an end to his column long ago. Too many editions and too many columns getting produced every week is my only excuse."

"It helped Warren's cause that the column was a favorite

with so many readers. And where would we be without readers, not to mention advertisers?"

Rob waved to the bartender. "I think you need another martini, Holly. Let me get us another round."

"Good idea!" Holly said as she finished the rest of her first. "Well, here's to Warren—wherever he is, and whoever he was."

CHAPTER TWENTY-FOUR

I n Rob's view, running a chain of weekly community newspapers was like jumping on a treadmill that started running early Monday morning and kept going until Friday afternoon. And then there were those times when the job ran all seven days of the week. But for all its frustrations, there were moments of unique pleasure when you stumbled onto a story that everyone else missed.

Rob was quickly coming to the conclusion that the mystery of Bradley's past might well be one of those overlooked, but nonetheless amazing, stories, made all the more shocking and relevant if a connection could be made between Warren's murder and his undiscovered past.

As more letters landed on Rob's desk asking why Grant Randolph was not in custody for the killing of Warren Bradley, the more Rob thought how ridiculous that idea was.

Unlike Bradley, Randolph had a well-documented past. From his childhood in Providence, Rhode Island, to his attending Brown University, to his developing one of SoHo's most successful art galleries, it was all there through the Internet, easily accessible.

On the other hand, Bradley's past disappeared like San Francisco behind a veil of summer fog. If indeed he was over seventy at the time of his death, then Warren was probably in his mid-forties when he arrived in Sausalito. Rob reasoned that Bradley must have had a hand in obscuring his past. Why else did he create a tangle of lies about his life, all of which led nowhere?

Late Saturday, a frustrated Holly called Rob and provided further reason for his growing suspicions. "Wow, Rob, you were right! I spent the day coming up with blanks on Bradley. This has to be a case of a name change, and it must have occurred outside of California because the state's database of application filings for name changes is pretty darn good. Unfortunately, California has nothing on the Warren Bradley we're looking for."

"Thanks, Holly. We're both on the same page in believing that something stinks about all this, and it's pretty clear at this point that Bradley played an active role in covering up his past. The big question is why?"

"When you or Eddie find out something nefarious about this guy, please let me know. And whatever you do, don't tell the Ladies of Liberty until after they erect that statue. I want to be there when they have to tear it down." Holly laughed at her own joke. "Ciao," she added quickly and clicked off.

Rob stared at the first few paragraphs of the story he was trying to cobble together on his late columnist. After writing and then abandoning four story openings, Rob reasoned it was time to talk with Eddie.

On Sunday morning, they met for breakfast at a café in the small town of Larkspur. Being ten miles north of Sausalito, there was a very slim chance that they would run into any of their neighbors, let alone someone curious enough to listen in on their conversation.

"From everything I can put together, Bradley didn't exist before he landed in Sausalito," Rob said with a shake of his head.

Eddie smiled. "I'm starting to think poor Warren might have been a bad little boy. Maybe something—or more accurately someone—finally caught up with the great chef."

"What do you guys do when you hit a wall like this? I mean, it's got to be a name change or something like that, right?"

"Pretty likely. Every year, more about us ends up online. Bradley probably wanted to hide from prying eyes, and he probably started hiding before the Internet became a go-to resource. Unless you're paying attention, there's an awful lot of information about us that leaks out from social media and search engines. Of course, that wasn't the case back when Warren arrived in Sausalito."

Rob took a sip of his coffee. "You must have a Plan B."

"Yep, and Plans C, D, and E. Whatever nastiness Bradley fell into, it's reasonably certain it happened before he arrived in Sausalito. But unfortunately, we can't trace him through any government fingerprint data bank. The killer might have kept Bradley's hands and the prints that went with them for that very reason. Therefore, we can't know if in the past he worked one of a dozen different jobs that they fingerprint people for as part of standard personnel procedures. Not to mention new government programs like the TSA's airport security pre-check."

"So, what's your next step?"

"I think it's time for us to take a little jog together—say, five-thirty tomorrow morning."

Rob groaned. "Why so early?"

"Because we're going on a little hunting expedition up to Warren Bradley's. When we were called to the scene and my two colleagues from the Sausalito PD scattered to different parts of the house, I 'accidentally' took a spare key to Warren's cottage that was sitting atop the refrigerator. I could go through channels, but A, I don't know what it is we're looking for, which is something you never want to tell your superiors; B, an authorized search means taking two or more of Sausalito's Keystone Cops along. Instead, I'm up for a little snooping while I'm off the clock."

"Can't we drive up there this evening? I can wait in the car while you snoop around."

"More convenient, for sure. But there's a good chance that a neighbor will see the lights on, or see a flashlight and call our friends at the SPD—which is exactly what we're trying to avoid."

"And why do we want to keep the SPD out of this?"

"Because, if you remember, its officers and staff are the original town gossips! How do you think Bradley got on the trail of everyone's favorite suspect, Grant Randolph, in the first place? I don't know which one of those chuckleheads babbled about Randolph's arrest for assaulting his wife, but I'll bet you a week's salary that was Warren's original source for his story. If we got caught up there, we'd be the talk of the town forty-eight hours later! We need to fly under the radar while we're there."

R ob watched the sky brighten over the East Bay as he strolled down his driveway Monday morning. He had just paused for a moment when Eddie came running up. The way they were dressed, they looked like any other early morning power joggers.

They took a circuitous route, winding through the Sausalito hills. Part of their jog took them along Glen Drive. They followed it as it curved uphill onto Santa Rosa Avenue, then onto San Carlos, Spencer, and finally onto Prospect.

By the time they had reached the end of Prospect, it was nearly six o'clock and they had come to the mutual conclusion that they should consider jogging the hills of Sausalito more often.

"Helluva workout," Eddie panted. Rob nodded breathlessly in agreement.

The sun was peeking up over the East Bay, and the air was sparkling fresh.

Eddie reached into his pocket. "Oh, damn! I forgot the key."

As the color drained out of Rob's face, Eddie punched him lightly on the chest. "I'm just screwing with you, man." He pulled the key out of his pocket and smiled. He then shifted his gaze toward the neighboring homes. After seeing that not a single soul was stirring, he murmured, "Let's do this."

Parts of the house were wrapped with the bright yellow CRIME SCENE tape that was put up the night Warren was wheeled away. It covered the door about six inches above the simple doorknob lock that provided the home's only security.

Eddie kneeled down below the tape, slipped the key in the lock, and smiled at Rob as it turned and popped open. He then reached into his pocket and pulled out two pairs of surgical footwear covers, and two pairs of blue nitrile gloves.

"Put these on, Robin," Eddie said.

"Whatever you say, Batman."

They slipped carefully under the yellow tape and into the house; quietly closing the single hinged French door behind them.

Warren's cottage held the chill of Sausalito's night air. Enough daylight came in through the windows to provide the needed amount of light.

Eddie's first suggestion was that they walk through each room of the small home and consider where they might want to begin their search. "I'd like to be out of here by seven at the latest. But, let me say, if anyone comes tapping on the door, from nosy neighbor to Sausalito PD, I do the talking. Agreed?"

"Absolutely! You got any idea what you'd say?"

"That's easy. If you see anyone pull up, or a neighbor comes walking toward the house, strip off your gloves and booties. We were jogging together and noticed that the front door was ajar. I stepped inside to see if anything seemed to have been disturbed before calling it in."

"Wow! You are smooth, Eddie."

"In my line of work, you better be ready to spread a little bullshit at a moment's notice."

"In my line of work as well! I guess we have more in common with politicians than we ever thought," Rob said with a smile. "Okay, tell me again what you think we might find."

"Bradley might have wanted, or needed, to obscure his past. But most people hold on to certain things out of sentimental attachment or any of a dozen other reasons. I doubt everything in his life that was more than twenty-five years old was thrown out. It could be one of a dozen different things. Maybe it's an original birth certificate or a picture of him with his parents or siblings. In other words, look for anything that gives us a key to who he was before he became the Warren Bradley the Ladies of Liberty adored."

They wandered separately through the cottage. The wood paneling throughout the house had absorbed the aromas of many meals created in the small, neatly arranged kitchen, which still showed the signs of Warren's last night of entertaining. Two dinner plates, two dessert plates, and two wine glasses had been washed, placed in the dish rack, and left there after his last supper.

"Interesting, isn't it, Rob? The killer wanted us to know that Bradley had a dinner guest. No prints anywhere in the place, and no DNA evidence on discarded food scraps, or cloth or paper napkins, but obvious signs that a guest had been here. I'm telling you this place was as clean as any murder scene I've ever seen. Of course, with the Sausalito police being the first here, there might have been a slice of chocolate cake on the sideboard that one of their geniuses ate."

"If they did, it was after I left and went home because, from the time they arrived, no one ever thought to go inside the cottage until the deceased's hands were discovered missing."

Eddie laughed. "I'm sorry I wasn't here until later. That must have been one memorable moment!"

"Trust me Eddie, it's one I'll never forget."

They wandered back and forth through the combined

living room, dining room, kitchen area, and then around the bedroom with the small nook that Warren used to write his now-infamous column.

Afterward, Eddie and Rob stood back to back and considered where they would look in the relatively brief time that they had left.

Eddie wanted to start by going through the Chippendale oak wood curio cabinet. It had a variety of plaques and awards from various cooking contests and "volunteer of the year" framed certificates from a variety of Sausalito organizations. He carefully slipped them out and looked behind each one.

Inside of one frame that had a back that quickly slipped off was the picture of a kid Eddie guessed to be about twelve to fourteen. From the washed-out colors of the photo and the clothing the boy was wearing, it was probably twenty-five years or older.

Perhaps it was a son Bradley left behind?

Eddie's curiosity was heightened when a second photo revealed another boy—maybe four to five years younger, sitting in the back of a rowboat tied to a crumbling wooden dock.

He slipped both photos into his pocket.

Rob's search focused on an antique mahogany bedroom dresser and the battered old Queen Anne desk in the bedroom nook. He took out each of the desk's two narrow and deep side drawers. One by one, he turned them over and emptied their contents onto the floor. He quickly looked through every scrap of paper, hoping to find something that placed Warren somewhere, anywhere, other than Sausalito.

He found nothing.

He piled the papers back into what he hoped was their

original drawers, but then he realized that it was highly unlikely anyone alive today would know what papers went where. Just knowing that he was a few feet from where Warren may have been suffocated and later mutilated sent a shiver down Rob's spine.

He pulled out the third drawer—the widest and flattest, from below the center of the desktop—when his hand felt something strange on the drawer's bottom, backside. It was enough to make Rob's heart skip a beat. Excitedly, he flipped over the drawer.

A blank white plastic card was taped to the aging wood.

"Eddie, get in here! I think I found something important."

Eddie came running. When he saw what Rob was indicating, he took the small penknife that was attached to his house keys and carefully cut the tape around the card's edges. On the flip side of the card was the photo of a man they both barely recognized as Warren Bradley, probably in his mid-thirties. This Warren had no gray hair, no bushy salt and pepper mustache, and no tired eyes. But after a few moments of careful consideration, they were both certain this was Warren, only several decades younger.

The card was an ID badge from the department of biomedical research at Northern Arizona University. There was no date of issuance on the card, but there was a name:

William Benedict.

They both stood and stared in silence for a few moments.

Finally, Eddie put his arm around Rob's shoulder and pulled him in close. "Rob, say hello to William Benedict. He must have had some shirts he liked with 'WB' on the cuffs. I guess he didn't want to give up his old initials." He handed his find to Rob: the photos of the two young boys. "Now, take a look at these! You're not the only one to come away with a prize."

"Do you think they might be Bradley's kids?"

"Could be," Eddie said. "Hopefully, William Benedict will be able to tell us who he was, and who these boys are as well."

"Eddie, let's get the hell out of here."

"Just what I was about to say."

Carefully they checked that everything was put back as they found it, with the only items removed being those only Warren Bradley likely knew were there all the time. Eddie relocked the door and they both removed their surgical shoe covers and gloves, which Eddie slipped back into his pocket.

"Remember when I told you that you have to keep pulling at all the different threads until you find the one string that causes all the others to unravel? In this case, let's hope William Benedict is that string."

When Rob got home, he quickly shaved, showered, and got ready to head down to the office for the official start of his workweek.

"First a break of dawn jog, then you're ready to hustle down to the office before eight? My God, you're a new man!" Karin said teasingly. But from her tone, he could tell she was curious about what he and Eddie had been doing since the first light of day.

Rob smiled innocently and waved as he went out the door. In truth, he was bursting to tell Karin about the discovery he and Eddie had made sixty minutes earlier, but he knew that no one could know about that for now—not even his life partner.

As usual, Holly was in the office before Rob arrived. She greeted him with the question: "What did you decide to do on the Bradley retrospective?"

"I have to punt. We'll pull together file photos and story clips of Warren doing his cooking and serving bit for every volunteer group in town. Other than that, as far as I can tell, the guy was dropped here one night by an alien spacecraft."

"That's a plausible theory. Still, you probably shouldn't put it into print."

"All I've got now is a senior citizen who was born twenty-five plus years ago. And I'm not making that my lead paragraph." Rob felt guilty holding back on Holly, particularly knowing how much the news regarding William Benedict would have thrilled and delighted her.

Rob couldn't imagine how big a story Eddie might uncover. At the same time, he had complete confidence in Eddie that, whatever the outcome of this strange case, he and his readers would be the first to know the whole story; hopefully in time for the next edition of *The Sausalito Standard*.

With that university ID badge in hand, Eddie was also confident that Warren's real story—and perhaps even the identity of his killer—were within reach. Finding William Benedict in Northern Arizona University's databank clinched it.

More shocking was his discovery of Benedict's arrest on a charge of homicide—something that for now, he needed to keep from Rob.

Eddie regularly had to remind himself that his closest

friend's chosen profession made it that much harder to share with him potentially explosive information. No matter what else he turned up, the very knowledge that Warren Bradley— the persistent persecutor of Grant Randolph, Carrie Kahn, and so many others—had been tried for homicide would be enough to have Rob aching to get to his keyboard and begin writing a blockbuster story. Expecting his friend to sit quietly on that information would have been like placing a boulder atop a volcano in the hope that it would stay put in an eruption.

CHAPTER TWENTY-FIVE

Four days after they searched Warren's home, Eddie got his department's approval for out-of-state travel expenses.

After landing in Phoenix, he planned on picking up a rental car and driving the three hours north on Interstate 17 to Flagstaff—home of NAU, Northern Arizona University.

Rob would have happily paid his expenses to go along, but faced with putting another week's editions on press, he waited anxiously for Eddie's call.

All day Friday, Rob had an edge in his voice.

"Maybe you should head over to Smitty's for an early end of the week happy hour," Holly groused after Rob snapped at her one too many times over a missing photo or a typo.

"You're probably right. I could use a beer, but I'm skipping it this week. Eddie had to go out of town on some work thing. I'm going straight home after work."

"Why don't you join me at the No Name for a drink?"

As grumpy as he'd been all day, she was owed at least an

end of the week cocktail. But then he remembered the rest of this weekend's itinerary. He shook his head. "Thanks, Holly, but Karin and I are going to try to leave by noon tomorrow for an overnight at her folks' place up in Calistoga. We've got errands to run before that, so we'll have to get an early start tomorrow."

"Okay, suit yourself. Maybe I'll get lucky and meet Mr. Right tonight."

That's not too likely, Rob thought, considering that the same gang can be found at the No Name Bar just about every night of the year.

"The first round is on me," he said, as he handed her a ten-dollar bill.

Holly snatched it up. "I should complain about your being grumpy more often," she giggled as she went out the door.

It was nearly five-thirty by the time Holly made the three-block walk up Bridgeway to her destination. She walked into the No Name and was unhappy to see the same old early evening crowd.

As busy as it already was, Holly was lucky to find a seat at the bar. She caught the bartender's attention—Alberto, a handsome thirty-something guy who worked behind the bar and made it a point to know all his customers.

"Hangar 1 martini, two olives, one onion—right, Holly?"

Holly gave Alberto a seductive wink. "I guess you know me, huh?"

As she waited a few moments for the bartender to work his magic, her eye caught a familiar face she had difficulty placing.

When Alberto put her drink down in front of her and asked with a warm smile if she needed anything else, Holly said, "Yes I do. How about the name of that cute guy over there, blue shirt, blond hair?"

"That's Chris Harding. He's a patrol officer with the Sausalito police."

She smiled. "Do you think I can get him to lock me up?"

"I guess that depends on how badly you behave," Alberto responded with a laugh and a wink as he hurried off to serve another customer.

Holly absentmindedly stirred her martini. Where had she seen Hottie Harding before? Oh yes—she'd met him and Officer Steve Hansen at the reception after Bradley's memorial service.

Eventually, Holly caught Chris's eye. They exchanged smiles and an air toast.

A few minutes later, Chris walked over to her side of the bar and stuck out his hand.

He had a firm but deliberately gentle grip. Holly liked his smile, along with the rest of him.

"I feel sure we've met before," Chris said.

"Well, Sausalito is such a small town that—"

"Wait a minute; I know where...It was at the reception after Warren Bradley's service." His smile faded. "That was a sad day, wasn't it? He was such a talented guy. Not mention a fantastic cook!"

"Yes, he was one in a million." Holly took it as a good sign that she didn't have to remind him exactly where and when they first met.

After a few minutes of small talk, Holly's mating mind clicked in. It confirmed her initial interest. Chris was probably mid-thirties, which made him a little younger, or a little older, than her—check. He had great features: blond hair, blue eyes, handsome face, and adorable dimples on his cheeks, which appeared each time he smiled—double check. And clearly, he had an impressive build underneath that soft blue cotton shirt he was wearing.

Yep, right age, good job, great body, and an adorable smile.

He was Holly's boyfriend trifecta.

Chris explained why he had made the move up from San Jose to Sausalito, and Holly told him that she worked at *The Standard.*

"I've heard a lot about the paper, but I haven't read it."

It was after Holly's second martini and Chris's second Jack Daniels and soda that he leaned into her and said, "You know, my place would be a lot quieter for us to talk than here."

Holly thought for a moment, and then said with a smile, "So would my place."

"Where is it?" Chris asked as he moved in close to be heard over the growing Friday night crowd.

"I'm on Caledonia Street, but truth be told I've got nosy neighbors."

"I'm renting a small guest cottage uphill on Easterby, that's just a couple of minutes away. And from what I hear, the local police are always on the lookout for DUIs."

"I guess you'd know, huh?" Holly said in a whisper followed by a soft kiss on his cheek.

Holly grabbed her purse and together they were out the door in a rush.

❀

Saturday was another beautiful day, as most are in Marin during California's dry season. Shortly before one, as Rob and Karin were finally getting together what they and the kids would need for their overnight in Calistoga, the phone rang.

It was Eddie.

"Hey man," Rob said. "You sound a little tired."

"Long night. But I'm at my departure gate, in Phoenix."

"Wow! That was fast."

"Saw all the folks I needed to see, first at NAU, and then Flagstaff PD, and even at the department of social services. Our late Mr. Bradley, known here as Mr. Benedict, had quite the backstory."

"Tell me more."

"I will after you pick me up outside the arrivals area at Oakland airport."

"But Karin and I are going with the kids up to her folks' place in Calistoga for the night," Rob explained, knowing he was desperate to hear about Eddie's trip.

"Hate to spoil your plans, pal, but we're going to make an arrest—probably early Monday—of a suspect in the killing of Warren Bradley. I think that after all the work you've done on this story, you'd certainly want to be there at the end."

"What time do you land?"

"Should be on the ground by three-forty-five. Southwest flight eight-oh-two."

"Sure, okay. I'll be on my cell. Just ring me when you're heading out of the terminal, and I'll pick you up at the curb."

"Okay, see you there."

"Eddie?"

"Yes?"

"Want to give me a hint?"

"Sorry, pal, there's no way I'm going to miss the expression on your face when you hear the rest of this story."

C hris and Holly slept in until just past noon. They kissed, first gently, and then passionately. Chris suggested that they go out for breakfast, but Holly insisted that he let her cook for him.

He agreed, and she dressed quickly and then took a brisk fifteen-minute walk down to the Marinship, and into Mollie Stone's Grocery, where she bought eggs, sausage, white cheddar cheese, and a Rustic Bakery sourdough polenta bread. She wasn't sure about Chris's taste in coffee, so she went for the top of the line, picking up a small bag of Kona Blue Mountain coffee beans.

On her way back to Chris's snug cottage, she walked along the waterfront. Whereas in the early 1940s this area, known as the Marinship, was teeming with shipbuilders serving America's war effort in the Pacific, now it provided a peaceful harbor for sailboats and houseboats.

Holly stopped herself from thinking how happy it made her waking up to find a handsome man next to her who seemed to adore her.

Holly loved his little place, and she was impressed at how neat he kept it. Chris was just stepping out of the shower when she walked back in. He wore nothing but a small yellow towel that was wrapped tightly around his waist. In the bright light of day, Holly could more fully appreciate the sculpted quality of his physique: flat abs, broad shoulders, and powerful arms.

She put down her groceries and wrapped her arms around her newly found love. "Where have you been all my life?"

"I was thinking the very same thing about you."

"To hell with breakfast," Holly said, as the two held each other, kissed passionately, and fell back into bed.

K arin insisted that Rob not feel guilty about the last-minute change of plans. "Don't worry. I'll take the kids up to Calistoga. They have their hearts set on seeing Grandpop and Nanna and I don't want to disappoint them. Besides, it sounds as if you're going to be busy working on your story for most of the weekend."

"Thanks, sweetie. What a break for us if Eddie has cracked the case and we're the first with the whole story! It'll put *The Standard* in a whole different league. The dailies will all be quoting our reporting instead of the other way around."

She kissed Rob on the cheek. "I'm excited for you, hon. And, frankly, it'd be wonderful to put an end to all this hysteria over the guilt or innocence of Grant Randolph. I can't imagine their relief in seeing all this craziness come to an end."

"G ood flight?" Rob asked Eddie as he tossed his overnight bag and briefcase on the back seat.

"That's not what you drove down here to ask."

"Gee, you really can see right through me."

"Let's go over to Francesco's, right outside the airport. It's off Hegenberger. I think they open at four. I'm starved, and I could go for some Italian comfort food and a double Scotch."

"I've got to wait until then?"

"Francesco's is five minutes from here. Besides, as I told you over the phone, I'm not going to miss the expression on your face when you hear this story. Hell, I might take a snap of your puss with my phone! I want to see if your chin can fall all the way to the floor."

"Okay, I won't say a word until we're seated. Hopefully, in the meantime, my head won't explode."

"I hope not; you're the one driving."

As Eddie slid into one of the restaurant's leather-upholstered black banquettes, he let out a sigh of relief. "I feel like I've been going nonstop for the last thirty-six hours."

"Sounds like it was worth it, though."

"That's an understatement." With a tired smile, Eddie waved down a waitress for, "A Johnnie Walker Black, on the rocks. Make it a double," he told her.

"Having the good stuff, I see."

"I deserve it."

Rob waited impatiently, sipping on water, while Eddie eased into his scotch and attacked a plate of lasagna.

When, finally, he had only a few bites left, Rob, who came only with an appetite for information, muttered, "Okay, give! I've been holding my breath for hours—no, make that days."

Eddie nodded, and put down his fork. "First, I met with

two of Benedict's co-workers, the only two who are still on staff from the time he worked there. Benedict was, shall we say, eased out of his position at NAU. There was quite a stink about that. He was living with a woman named Elaine Hayden. They met at NAU; she worked in student services."

"And?"

"She died just a year after Benedict moved in with her. It was a violent death, and the Coconino County prosecutor's office tried her boyfriend, Sausalito's superstar gourmet chef, for murder one. But based on the evidence, that was perhaps an overreach. They probably could have sold the jury on a manslaughter conviction."

"How did she die?"

"Broken neck," Eddie said with a wince. "She fell down a flight of steps in her own home."

"Wow!"

"Bradley—I mean Benedict claimed it was an accident. The Flagstaff police and the county sheriff's department had reason to believe it was a homicide."

"Why was that?"

"Turns out that the older boy in one of those two pictures we found was Hayden's son, from a previous marriage. The younger one was a foster kid who was placed in the house at the age of six, around eighteen months before Hayden's death."

"But what made the cops think Hayden's fall was anything other than an accident? Did her kids witness the fall?"

"Let me back up a bit. You see, two weeks before she died, Elaine Hayden went to child welfare services claiming that Benedict had molested both boys. Of course, Benedict denied everything. He insisted that both boys fabricated the stories because he was strict with them, and it was their way of driving a wedge between him and their mother."

"Then what?"

"Child services brought in therapists to talk with both the boys. The older one, James, who had just turned twelve at the time, said he had been molested on and off during the time Benedict lived in the home. But Topher, the youngest of the two, denied ever having been touched by Benedict. Interestingly enough, however, it was the younger one who told investigators that our Mr. Bradley had pushed Hayden down the steps, but the defense shredded the kid's story on the witness stand."

"What about the older brother?"

"Bad luck for the prosecutor, great luck for Benedict. James was at a sleepover the night his mother died. He would likely have been a much more convincing witness than the little guy. He did give child services quite a credible description of Benedict's behavior from what I could tell reading through the trial transcript, but getting a murder one conviction on Benedict, based on the testimony of a seven-year-old foster kid who came from a very challenging background, well, that was a very tall order."

"What a sad story," Rob said shaking his head.

"The jury deliberated for four days and then voted for acquittal. If it had been a hung jury, Bradley could have been re-tried. Unfortunately, the prosecutor went for all the marbles and walked away with zip.

"Despite being acquitted, Benedict lost his job."

"Couldn't he have sued NAU?" Rob asked.

"Yes. But I guess in this case; Bradley must have felt he had just beaten a hangman's noose, and thought it a better idea to thank God he was a free man. So he didn't make a big fuss about the dismissal, he just got the hell out of town determined to start his life over again."

"Where did he go after Flagstaff?"

"One of the guys in the sheriff's office took a particular liking to the boys, both of whom had been placed in separate homes after Hayden's death. Like a lot of small counties, Coconino has limited resources, but the sheriff did his best to keep tabs on Benedict. The last he heard, he was living a thousand miles east of Flagstaff, in Tulsa, Oklahoma. That's where I tracked down the name change he filed to go from Benedict to Bradley."

"Doesn't law enforcement keep a national database for child predators?"

"Yes. But remember, he was acquitted of the murder. As for the molestation accusation, somehow the new name became his loophole on that score." Eddie sighed. "At least the kids had been placed far away from Benedict, regardless of what he did or did not do. Things calmed down, new cases started up, and old cases began to fade into the past. Flagstaff was simply glad to be rid of William Benedict. The city and county workers involved in the case were not overly concerned about where he went, as long as it was very far from their jurisdiction."

"Any idea what happened to the kids?"

"Hayden's son, the one who was twelve at the time of her death, later died of a drug overdose. Poor kid! From what I read in his file, he had a pretty miserable life after his mom died. He went to live with Hayden's parents but fell in with a bad crowd. I would love to have spoken with him about William Benedict before he became the Warren Bradley we knew."

"What about the younger boy, and how does any of this tie into Bradley's murder?"

"I'm getting to that. The younger kid bounced from one foster home to another. At fifteen, by some miracle, he caught a break. He wound up in San Jose with a great family and stopped acting out. He went to San Jose State, studied criminal justice like yours truly, and his foster care dad got him a position with the San Jose police department. Could have been a happy ending, but..."

"But what?"

"You don't know the name of that troubled little seven-year-old boy. Remember little Topher who got chewed up by Benedict's defense team? He decided to take the last name of his San Jose family: Harding. He now goes by his given name, Christopher, you know, Chris, as in Chris Harding."

"WHAT?" Rob, realizing how loud he had said that single word, grimaced. Fortunately, before five o'clock, Francesco's was still mostly empty.

"The new kid with the Sausalito PD? You mean that Chris?"

"Sí, señor, one and the same. Patrol Officer Chris"—Eddie said the last name slowly—"Harding."

For a few moments, Rob remained speechless. He mumbled in a low voice, "Oh, my God," as he flagged down their waitress and ordered a vodka tonic. "This is just incredible! I don't suppose there's any chance this is an enormous coincidence?"

"Anything is possible, Rob. You might get a call from the Pope tomorrow saying he can't keep the Vatican newspaper running without you, but I doubt that's going to happen."

"Jesus, Mary, and Joseph! So, what's next?"

"Chris will most likely be arrested Monday morning before going to work. A request for an arrest warrant has to be presented to one of the county's judges, and then I'll have to contact SPD so that two officers can accompany me while I make the arrest. At least one of those officers will ride along with Harding while he is processed through, and into the county jail to await an arraignment hearing.

"Instead of going to the suspect's home, I could go to Sausalito police headquarters, but that might get messy. That many of their crew standing around with firearms? I'd hate to see their squad room turn into a circular firing squad."

Rob frowned. "Won't going through channels, as you put it, take time? What if he gets wind of the arrest? He's got a lot of buddies on the force, and none of them can keep their damn mouths shut. He may vanish."

"In the weeks since Bradley's killing, he has gone about his normal life. I guess he assumes he got away with murder, particularly with better than half of the town demanding Randolph's arrest and the Sausalito PD maintaining a twenty-four-hour watch on the Randolphs' empty house. If Harding were going to run, he would have skedaddled by now."

"I guess you're right." Rob felt his head spinning with how much he had suddenly learned about Warren Bradley.

"Oh, I don't want to forget to mention!" Eddie said, "You and I have to make another run early tomorrow."

"Where now?"

"Where else? Back to Bradley's cottage. I think there is one little gem we might have missed."

"What's that?"

"Oh, come on, Rob. You don't want me to take *all* the surprise out of this, do you?"

CHAPTER TWENTY-SIX

Before dropping Eddie off at his house, both agreed to meet Sunday morning at that same ungodly hour: five-thirty in the morning. Rob ached at the thought of missing a chance to sleep in, especially with the family out of the house and Karin not pushing him to get the kids ready for church. The silver lining of not spending the weekend with the family was getting an extra two hours or more of sleep Sunday morning. Now that was gone.

The excitement of closing the Bradley case, however, not to mention the anticipated embarrassment this news would soon cause Alma Samuels and her Ladies of Liberty—was more than enough to compensate Rob for any amount of lost sleep.

The moment Rob was alone, visions of headlines danced in his head. "The Secret Life of Warren Bradley Revealed," was his favorite for now, but there was plenty of time to create others before his Tuesday afternoon on-press deadline. If the arrest occurred on Monday, the dailies, broadcast, and their Internet pages would all beat him by a day with the fact that an arrest had been made. But where their stories ended, Rob's would begin.

The story of William Benedict was all his.

Rob got into bed by ten and set his alarm for five. He drifted off to sleep, as excited as a kid the night before summer vacation.

Holly was amazed. She had floated through all of Saturday on a cloud. Chris was not only a gentleman; he was tender, considerate, and attentive to her needs.

Saturday night, the newly minted twosome decided to leave their love nest to go to the movies. Afterward, they went to Marin Joe's, famous for great burgers and creamed spinach. The two kissed and held hands while sharing the same side of a booth.

Holly felt sure she had at last found her Mr. Right.

Over dinner, for the first time, they spoke about their jobs. Chris shared his view that Sausalito was beautiful, but a significant change from the fast-paced world of San Jose. "Let's just say that your shift went by a lot faster in San Jose than it does in Sausalito."

"Do you miss it?" Holly asked.

"In some ways, I honestly do. You felt more like a cop there."

"And in Sausalito?"

"I feel like a cross between a school safety guard and a tour guide for visitors."

Holly laughed.

He gave her a quick kiss. "So, what's it like, working at *The Standard*?"

"It's pretty cool. It can get crazy, but I'm used to the pace. And, let me tell you, the days go pretty fast when something is going on all the time."

"That's the way things used to be for me in San Jose. Has coverage of the Bradley killing been keeping you busy?"

"Yes and no. You have to remember—we put out four separate publications that land in homes on different days of the week in different areas of Marin. Bradley's a huge story in Sausalito, but not very important in the other towns. He was the walking definition of a local celebrity." She shrugged. "What do you think? Who knocked off the old busybody?"

Chris laughed. "Busybody! That's a good one. I heard some guy wrote a letter to your paper, calling Bradley the 'gossiping gourmet.' Down at headquarters, he was just a nice old guy who made the staff great lunches once a month."

"Some people thought he was a real pain in the butt."

"Do you think this art commission guy Randolph killed Bradley? Seems like half the town, or more, believe that."

"I thought there was a good chance of that at first, but I don't know now."

"What's changed your mind?"

"My boss, Rob, has been trying to put together a piece about Bradley's life, but he's had a hard time finding out anything about Warren's life before he came to Sausalito."

Chris shrugged. "Must be frustrating. If your boss isn't getting anywhere, maybe the paper should just put the story aside. It sounds like you've got enough to do every week without having to play detectives."

"You know, sweetie, I think he would do that if it wasn't for

Alma Samuels and her Ladies of Liberty breathing down his neck."

"Oh," Chris frowned, deep in thought, as he munched on a few French fries. "I hear she's got a lot of clout around town. I know Chief Petersen hates it when she calls."

"Believe me; Alma deserves to be whacked over the head with a shovel."

"Wow, you've got a lethal side to you! I better watch myself."

Holly squeezed Chris's leg as she teasingly fed him one of her fries. She leaned in and whispered, "Oh, you don't know the half of it, baby! I can be a dangerous lady when I want."

"I'm starting to find that out," He nodded toward the door. "I think it's time we get back to my place."

Holly signaled the waiter for a check. Minutes later they were driving back to their love nest.

Rob woke before sunrise. He did some warm-up stretches while waiting for Eddie to appear. Before long, the two of them were back, following the same circuitous route they had taken just six days before.

Jogging down the final half mile along Prospect, Rob realized that in thirty minutes they had not passed a single car, hiker, jogger, or dog walker.

"At six on a Sunday morning, this town is really dead," he exclaimed. "Seems like we're the only ones dumb enough to be up at this hour."

"Don't you love it? I think we might want to start doing this a few days a week," Eddie suggested.

"Fine with me, as long as it's not on a day when I can sleep in," Rob muttered.

"Sorry about the early start with the kids being gone and all, but I'm hoping we'll strike gold a second time."

Rob chuckled. "May the Gods of law and order be with us."

Eddie winked. "We're on a roll, buddy. And I'm feeling lucky today."

Once inside, they again donned their surgical booties and nitrile gloves.

"Okay, Sherlock, what are you looking for this time?" Rob asked.

"When we were last here, I'd hoped to find something substantial, so I rushed through a lot of other stuff. I know I can bullshit my way around why we're here if we get caught, but I would prefer not to be in that position."

"And?"

"During our last visit I quickly flipped through that big binder over there on the kitchen counter next to the Cuisinart. It's filled with recipes, alongside which Bradley scribbled a lot of little notes in the margins. It mostly looked like names and dates, or additions and deletions of different ingredients. It would have been too much to cover in too little time, so I put the book aside and went looking at more likely hiding places, thinking that Bradley wasn't going to place anything from his past in there. Yesterday, while flying back to Oakland, I tried to remember what it was that Chris Harding told us about Bradley during the reception after the memorial service. Suddenly it came to me: it was how much he enjoyed that caramel chicken. Remember? Warren made it the day of the last luncheon he served down at the Sausalito PD."

"You're right, Eddie. He did mention that chicken."

"If he managed to get himself invited for dinner, perhaps that's what Bradley cooked. I want to see if he scribbled anything in the margin alongside that particular recipe."

"Wow! You're smarter than I realized."

"Thank you, kind sir. Now, go over to the door and keep an eye out for any of the neighborhood snoops while I spend a little time in the late chef's kitchen."

"I'm on it," Rob said, as he positioned himself to the side of the ancient French door.

Eddie said a little prayer as he opened the old binder with frayed corners. He turned the pages carefully, many of which had yellowed over time and stiffened with the grease that inevitably was absorbed when paper sits so close to a kitchen range.

The sections all started with a tab but were not themselves arranged alphabetically. Through the C's, Eddie went page by page, past the Clams Oreganata, and the Clam Chowder, the Couscous with Garbanzo Beans, and then a half dozen chicken recipes from the making of chicken sausage to Chicken Parmesan. Nearly every page had a date on it. Many of them had several. Eddie hoped that the book doubled as a kind of diary, reminding Warren how many times he'd made a particular recipe and for whom. Some notes said things like, "Alma's favorite," or "Women's League Holiday Luncheon."

When he came to the page that held the recipe for Caramel Chicken, the last note was "Sausalito PD," and the date of that final lunch, but there was no date after that.

"Damn it, there's nothing here," Eddie pounded his fist down on the counter.

"Maybe he never got the chance to write it down," Rob replied.

"Yeah, that could be. Still, it would have been sweet to have had one last nail in Harding's coffin."

"Wait a minute," Rob said suddenly, "Harding also mentioned pasta with veal, sausage, and porcini ragu."

"How the hell did you remember that?"

"Because I thought it sounded great. I suggested to Karin that we should try making it one night."

"What the hell, it's worth a try," Eddie said as he reopened the book.

For several more minutes he methodically turned over each page in the binder and then:

"BINGO," Eddie exclaimed too loudly, he quickly realized.

Alongside his pasta recipe, there was one last entry: *Chris Harding.*

Underneath the name, Warren wrote the date. It was the night he died.

"Something tells me you got it," Rob said.

Eddie pulled his phone out of his nylon running jacket and snapped a photo of the page.

"Let's get the hell out of here," Eddie said. "It's time for me to get a warrant for Chris Harding's arrest."

By the time Rob walked back in his front door—just a few minutes after seven—he was no longer interested in sleep. The sky was bright blue, but the streets of Sausalito were still quiet. The house was blessedly silent as well. Karin and the kids were likely still tucked in and fast asleep at her folks' place.

There were so many intriguing places for Rob to start this

story. How should he explain to his readers the mystery of William Benedict's life and Warren Bradley's death?

He was indecisive for a time, knowing the story had many points of entry. But, as he'd learned after years of turning out one story after another, there are times when you start writing and allow the story to take shape as you move forward. There was always time for taking a second, third, and fourth pass. Now was the best time to start putting words on a page.

With each new sentence, Rob could feel the weight of the mystery lifting off of him. His final deadline would be Tuesday afternoon. Even with news of the arrest of Chris Harding almost certainly breaking the morning before *The Standard* would arrive in-home, Rob was now fully confident that only his readers would have the full story.

He was so busy working away at his laptop that he hadn't realized it was going on nine. He decided he would wait until ten before giving Holly a call. Whatever else, Rob was sure that his longtime assistant would fall off her feet when she learned that Warren Bradley's killer was a Sausalito police officer.

CHAPTER TWENTY-SEVEN

R ob called Holly's home number precisely at ten. Having no luck, he tried her cell, but again there was no answer. He was disappointed, but it was okay; he had enough on his plate and Holly had little enough downtime from her average workweek.

Through Sunday afternoon, he shaped, changed, and re-worked his story. Shortly before five in the afternoon, Karin returned home with the children. Rob kissed her like she had been gone for a month. "I'm going to put on a movie for the kids. You and I have to talk."

When he told Karin his news, he wasn't surprised that she sat there for a time utterly speechless.

"I knew the butler didn't do it, Warren could never afford one," Karin proclaimed with the crooked smile that first caught Rob's interest and led him to, in his uniquely awkward way, ask her out on a date.

After hearing the outcome of the mystery, Karin was happy

for Eddie, thrilled for Rob, and pleased that the shadow of guilt would soon be lifted from Grant Randolph.

"Holly said for years that Warren Bradley was a creepy guy. That gal was spot on! I guess she's a pretty good judge of character. Speaking of Holly, what does she think of all this?"

"I've been trying her since ten this morning, but I've had no luck."

"Maybe she finally got smart, and she's hiding out. You can't blame the poor thing for wanting a little peace, given how hard she works all week." Having done Holly's exhausting weekly routine for several years, Karin knew this better than anyone, other than Rob.

After dinner, Rob asked Karin if she objected to his walking down to the office. "I have to clear some items off my desk so that I can spend most of Monday and Tuesday before press time getting the Bradley story as good as I can make it."

"Of course I don't mind," Karin said. "I know what a huge week this is going to be for you. I'm very happy for you, and I'm proud of the way you and Eddie worked together. You're quite a team."

By seven on a Sunday evening in downtown Sausalito, nearly all of the day visitors have traveled back to San Francisco, leaving the town once again to its citizens.

Rob walked along Bridgeway toward his office on Princess Street. He passed cafes busy with diners, street cleaners sweeping up after another busy weekend, and bike rental kiosk operators closing up their stands and tallying their weekend profits. As he walked by the No Name Bar, he stopped in for a moment.

Since I'm here, it's worth a shot, Rob thought, as he stopped, turned, and went inside. The place was starting to fill with the usual after dark locals. Rob did a quick look around and was disappointed not to see Holly.

"Rob," he heard a voice say. He turned and saw Alberto standing behind him.

"Got the night off?" Rob asked.

"Just finished working the day shift. You looking for Holly?"

"Yes. I was hoping she might be here."

"No, I haven't seen her since Friday. It was pretty funny."

"What was?" Rob asked.

"She and that new cop in town were sitting at the bar, making goo-goo eyes at each other. I think she's landed a keeper," Alberto smiled as he flashed Rob a thumb's up. "Anyway, they both beat it out of here—must have been around nine Friday night, and I haven't seen either of them since."

Trying to remain calm, Rob asked, "You don't mean Chris Harding, do you?"

"Yeah, Chris. Seems like a great guy," Alberto called out as Rob rushed out the door.

A few minutes later, Rob was at his desk. This could be bad, he thought, as he took a deep breath and collected himself before calling Eddie.

"What the hell do you want?" Eddie said, only half joking on a Sunday night.

"Are you sitting down?"

"No, but I could be. What's up?"

"I've been trying to find Holly all day, with no luck."

"That's no big deal, given that it's the weekend."

"I just saw Alberto down at the No Name. He last saw Holly Friday night. She left the bar—*with Chris Harding*. She hasn't been seen since."

"That's not good! Where are you right now?"

"Down at the office."

"I'll be right down."

After checking in with Rob, Eddie went to Holly's apartment on Caledonia Street. He got no answer when he rang her doorbell, so he knocked on the neighbors' doors at either side of her unit. Both reported having not seen Holly for the past two days.

Eddie had gotten Chris Harding's address earlier on Sunday when he began his paperwork for an arrest warrant. He drove over to Easterby and parked on the opposite side of the street from Chris's one-bedroom cottage. He made sure that his unmarked car was far enough away from any streetlight that could illuminate the interior of his vehicle. With binoculars, he focused in on the cozy home's interior.

There was a light on in the kitchen. Before long, Eddie saw Holly walk in, stir a pot on the stove and taste whatever it was she was cooking. As she stirred, Chris, shirtless, came up behind her, pulled her hair to one side, and nuzzled her neck. Holly turned, and they kissed.

Looks more like a scene out of *Love Story* than *Psycho*, Eddie thought. She is going to be disappointed when we lock up her new boyfriend!

Eddie reviewed his options, all of which needed to be

considered. There was an excellent chance that the arrest, scheduled for seven-thirty the following morning, would go off without a hitch. Holly wasn't in any immediate danger. At the moment, she was more of a love slave than a hostage.

Still, anything could go wrong. After all, Holly was shacked up with a man who had committed a brutal murder. And, for that matter, Eddie could find himself in serious trouble if one of his favorite people—crazy, lovable Holly—was harmed.

Eddie sat in the dark and kept an eye on the cottage as he thought about his next step. He chose the middle path between being overly cautious and disregarding an innocent civilian's safety. He arranged to have a deputy in an unmarked sheriff's department vehicle park across the street and remain there until Harding's scheduled arrest.

As Eddie's relief arrived, he headed home for what would undoubtedly be a fitful night's sleep.

Rob came back and was greeted by Karin, who immediately asked, "Why do you look so worried?" Rob came close to answering honestly, sharing his concerns about Holly, but then changed course.

"I want to get this story in the best shape possible. After this, it's back to reporting on guest speakers at the senior center and design review board meetings."

"Oh, honey!" Karin said as she reached up to kiss him on the cheek, "Maybe you'll get lucky, and in a few months someone else will get murdered."

"You mean, like one of the Ladies of Liberty?"

"If gossiping gourmets are getting knocked off, I suppose anything is possible."

Just before they turned off their lights, Rob got a text message from Eddie: "Easterby, 7:30 tomorrow morning. Walk halfway up the block and then hang back."

Neither Rob nor Eddie slept well that night.

CHAPTER TWENTY-EIGHT

Shortly before seven-thirty Rob walked into the 7-Eleven at the corner of Bridgeway and Easterby and got a cup of their usual burned and nearly tasteless coffee. As he stood outside the old wreck of a building, he looked up the block just as a black SUV with four large white letters printed on the side turned and headed up the block.

The SWAT armored vehicle stopped halfway up between where Rob stood and Chris Harding's cottage. No police personnel got out; the vehicle just waited there. One minute later, two Sausalito police cars went up the block and pulled up alongside the SWAT vehicle.

Two residents came out on their stoops and said in near unison, "What's going on?" The patrol officers waved them back inside. As the neighbors went back in, shut and locked their doors, Eddie's old unmarked black Plymouth rode past and stopped in front of Chris Harding's small cottage.

So far, so good, Eddie thought, as he walked up the small rise of the driveway and went around back to the small red cottage's only door, which faced in the opposite direction of the street. Placing his hand just inside his jacket, Eddie unsnapped his shoulder holster and removed his gun, but kept it hidden from sight.

Just as Eddie was about to knock, he heard the top bolt slide back. Eddie took a deep breath. As he often did at a moment like this, he thought about Sharon and his young son, Aaron. He all but laughed out loud when he saw Holly standing in the doorway alone, dressed, ready for work, and brushing her hair. She greeted Eddie with a smile.

"Hi, Eddie, what are you doing here?"

"Is Chris here?"

"Yeah, but sleepyhead is still snoozing. He doesn't have to go to work until one today. Meanwhile, I've got to get moving. I'm sure it's going to be another busy week with all this Bradley stuff still on the front burner."

Eddie put his index finger up to his lips and signaled her to come outside. She did but with a look of complete bewilderment. "Stay right here, and don't move."

Eddie slipped inside and saw Chris shirtless, sound asleep on his back. Quietly as he could, Eddie cuffed Chris's right hand to the side of the old iron rail headboard, and to his relieved amazement, Harding continued his light rhythmic snoring.

He then went back out as Holly, who was still attempting to tame her curly black hair, asked, "What's up, copper?"

Eddie took Holly by the arm and walked her around to the front of the driveway, where two armed SWAT officers moved her quickly away from the property.

Rob, who had been standing fifty yards down the road talking with two Sausalito patrol officers, walked up to Holly and slipped his hand around her arm. "I've got her from here, fellas. I'll take her back to her place."

Holly, looking bewildered. "What in the hell is going on, Rob?"

"They're arresting Chris Harding for the murder of Warren Bradley."

Her eyes grew wide. "Oh, no! That can't be! He's—he's such a sweet guy!"

"Come on, Holly," Rob said. "I have a few things I've wanted to tell you since early yesterday."

Chris woke up a few minutes later to find Holly gone and his bed surrounded by a SWAT team, two Sausalito patrol officers, and Eddie.

"Not good, huh?" were Chris's first words as he pulled on his cuffs.

"No, not good, buddy," Eddie responded.

"Where's Holly?

"Back out there, still looking for Mr. Right."

CHAPTER TWENTY-NINE

The news of Chris Harding's arrest for the murder of Warren Bradley was an even bigger shock to Sausalito society than the killing of the gossiping gourmet.

The evening television news gave it ninety seconds. The San Francisco papers put it below the fold. And the county's one daily, *The Independent*, had a headline that read:

Sausalito Police Officer Arrested in Slaying of Local Chef and Columnist

By Tuesday, the story was placed on the back burner awaiting a trial and a jury verdict. That same day, Rob's office phone rang incessantly. For the citizens of Sausalito, the arrest of Chris Harding created more questions than answers.

Rob finished that week's Sausalito edition with Karin's help —as Holly spent Monday and Tuesday in bed with a box of tissues and what she insisted was the worst hangover of her life.

Dozens of phone messages and email questions went unanswered, including two from Alma, who left one voicemail pleading with Rob for answers.

Wednesday morning, as mail carriers across Sausalito dropped that week's edition of *The Standard*, all their questions were answered.

As the Ladies of Liberty, the Siricas, arts commission members, and countless others in the tight-knit circle of Sausalito's friends and frenemies opened their weekly paper, they found that Rob had fulfilled the charge Alma had given him: "Lift every rock to see what evil lurks beneath."

Alma shuddered with horror as she read *The Sausalito Standard's* headline:

Homicide and Arrest Reveal the Secret Life of Warren Bradley

For Warren's staunchest admirers, the story was a tsunami of bad news. It erased all they imagined they knew about the man and left only bitter facts in its wake.

There was William Benedict's trial for the killing of Elaine Hayden; the charges of pedophilia; the heartbreaking story of Hayden's son, James, that was followed by the equally tragic tale of young Chris Harding.

The sum of which redefined Warren Bradley's place in Sausalito's long history of heroes and villains.

B y the time he came up for trial, Chris Harding had been transformed into a poster child for neglected and molested foster children. Those fortunate enough to win one of the few available seats at the Marin County Courthouse wept along with jurors as Chris's legal team retold his story, starting with the day William Benedict entered his life, and concluding with the day he ended Warren Bradley's life.

"But, why the hands, Mr. Harding? Why did you sever the hands of Mr. Bradley?" the prosecutor asked.

"I loved my brother James and my foster mother Elaine, even though I knew them for too little time. After they were gone from my life, I was handed off from one awful foster home situation to another. For years, I thought about Benedict's hands. Those hands pushed Mrs. Hayden down a flight of stairs. Those hands molested me and my brother, James."

"But Mr. Harding, at age seven, you testified that Mr. Benedict had not molested you."

"I was just a small boy terrified by everything that had happened. I was separated from James and placed in a different children's shelter. One of the boys there told me that if I said I had been molested, other kids and adults would make fun of me. But, just like James, Benedict molested me as well. I hated the memory of his filthy hands touching me even more than I hated him," Chris insisted, as he broke down in sobs that echoed from every corner of the courtroom. Half of the jurors choked back tears.

After his testimony, the judge declared a recess in the proceedings for the balance of the day.

Just as the prosecution's missteps in Flagstaff helped set

William Benedict free, the outcome for Chris Harding was equally fortunate.

By the time the trial neared its conclusion, the jury, angered by what they had heard from a long line of experts, was in all but open rebellion against the prosecution. The district attorney struck a deal with the defense: Chris Harding would plead not guilty by reason of temporary insanity and be placed in a state prison for a period of one year. At the end of that year, a court-appointed psychiatrist would determine if he should be allowed to re-enter society.

CHAPTER THIRTY

Rob's coverage of the murder, arrest, and trial of Chris Harding earned him a feature story in *The New Yorker* magazine. The piece was entitled, "The Secret Life of the Gossiping Gourmet."

Chris agreed to be interviewed for the article, which gave Rob an exclusive story of great interest to his hometown's readers. Rob hoped the remaining questions he had about this strange story would finally be answered.

Harding was being held in the psychiatric unit of a state prison located just north of the City of Santa Rosa, in Sonoma County. Rob walked in and met him in a private room that the jail had provided for their use. Chris looked relaxed and at peace with himself.

One guard sat quietly in a far corner of the room. No one seemed particularly concerned that there would be any sudden acts of violence. Nevertheless, Rob, who was only accustomed to interviewing people who had made hurtful comments about their fellow citizens, was still uneasy. Fortunately, Chris Harding's relaxed smile and comfortable manner made Rob quickly forget how dangerous he'd once considered him to be.

"How did you know that Warren Bradley wouldn't recognize you when you met him as an adult for the first time?" Rob began.

"I wondered about that. But when I sat next to him for an hour at the monthly department luncheon, I knew that wouldn't be a problem. I guess I shouldn't have been too surprised. The last time I was in his presence, I was seven. When I expressed interest in learning how to cook, he eagerly offered to give me private lessons." Chris winced. "It was obvious that he welcomed the opportunity to be alone with me. I knew then that I'd easily have my chance."

"Why did you decide to share with Warren the domestic violence call you responded to up at the Randolphs'?"

"That whole thing was like a gift from the gods. When I was called to the Randolphs' home, I knew I had some gossip that Bradley would find impossible to resist. It played out better than I could have imagined. When Grant Randolph almost cold-cocked Bradley in front of half the town on opera night, I knew I'd never get a better chance. Besides everything he had written about Randolph in *The Standard*, here you have the guy looking like he's ready to beat the creep to a bloody pulp. I played it cool, but I knew this was my best chance. The next day I called Bradley from a pay phone and asked if he had the time to give me a cooking lesson that week. He made a big deal about my being his 'savior,' and he was only too happy to give me some pointers on cooking."

"How in the world did you track Bradley down in the first place? He did a reasonably good job of covering up his past. I should know, Holly and I spent an entire weekend trying to track him down and got nowhere."

"While I was with the San Jose PD, I took a long weekend to visit Flagstaff. Mrs. Hayden had a friend who worked at the Coconino County clerk's office. She babysat for me a few times. Nice lady. I arranged to take her to lunch the day I arrived in town and asked if anyone had ever heard anything more about Benedict. She knew through the sheriff's office that he had settled in Tulsa and filed a name change going from Benedict to Bradley. Of course, that was years earlier. I tracked Bradley from Oklahoma back here to California. I finally located him in Sausalito. I put my name on a waiting list for an opening with the Sausalito PD and got hired six months later. The fact that Bradley made those volunteer lunches for the department was another stroke of good luck. But either way, I would have tracked him down. Small towns are not an easy place to blend into the crowd. And with Bradley turning himself into a minor celebrity it was that much easier."

"Sounds like you had wanted to kill Benedict for a very long time."

"You might say it was a cross between a fantasy and an obsession."

One last question had made Rob more curious than any other. "You almost got away with the perfect crime. You left the house clean of prints. From what Eddie Austin says there were no obvious signs of a homicide until you decided to chop off Bradley's hands. I know you spoke at the trial about your severing his hands, but I still feel there is more to the story. Is there?"

"Over the past twenty-five years, I'd imagined killing Benedict a thousand times in a hundred different ways. That night,

I kept refilling his glass with wine in the hope that it would put him into a sound sleep. It worked just as I had hoped. By the time I put the pillow over his head, I don't think he had become aware that he was unable to breathe until moments before he lost consciousness. There was no struggle. Afterward, I went around cleaning up everything I had touched and tossed in a plastic bag any trace of my DNA—napkins and such."

"No one would have known this was a murder," Rob said softly.

"I realized that," Chris grimaced. "As I was getting ready to leave, I looked at him and thought how peaceful he looked. I killed him, but what if I had done such a good job that the story of his life ended with people all talking about this good man who did all this great volunteer work, and died peacefully in his sleep? I imagined all those little old ladies telling me what a great guy dear Warren was! And that's when I snapped. I grabbed that expensive meat cleaver off the counter and whacked off his hands—and I certainly enjoyed doing that. I was sure the world would ask one simple question: 'Why did this happen to poor Warren?'"

It was chilling to Rob how logical an utterly insane act could sound.

On the hour-plus ride back to Sausalito, Rob kept thinking: *What in the world would I have done?*

A foster child finally placed in a loving home, and then it all turns into a nightmare.

Your new mom is dead, the new big brother you thought

you had is now out of your life; you're taken from one home to another, and you have only one thought: Someday I will destroy that man.

There were two things Rob wanted to do when he arrived back home. First, hold and hug his two young children as he never had before. Second, be thankful for Karin, their home, and all the other beautiful aspects of his life, which he too often took for granted.

Three months later the article's release in *The New Yorker* was celebrated at the No Name Bar.

"I'll bet when you were covering the two-year debate over improvements to Sausalito's dog park, you never thought this would happen!" Holly said as she lifted her glass high for a toast. "Here's to a great writer, a good friend, and a reasonably decent boss."

"So, Holly, will you be resurrecting your relationship with Chris Harding after the shrinks say he's free to go?" Eddie asked.

Holly shrugged. "He's a terrific guy, and certainly easy on the eye. It's tragic what happened to him, but I don't think we have a future together."

"Why not, Nancy Drew?"

"I can give you ten reasons," Holly said as she raised both her hands and wiggled her fingers in Eddie's face.

He gave a long laugh and said, "You can't give a guy a hand when he needs it most?"

Holly shook her head adamantly. "I'd rather appear small-minded with hands, than broadminded without them."

I n remarkably little time Warren Bradley's memory was purged from the carefully crafted histories of Sausalito.

"He deceived us!" Alma declared. She forbade the mention of his name in her presence. In fact, she and the Ladies of Liberty never spoke again of the man she had once greatly admired. The contributions gathered for Warren's memorial statue were returned to the donors without a note of thanks or explanation.

Just days after Chris Harding's arrest, Grant and Barbara Randolph came back to their lovely cottage by the bay.

Within two weeks, they received invitations to a half-dozen gatherings. It was surprising and gratifying for both of them to witness their resurrected social standing inside Sausalito's smart set.

Nevertheless, a year after Warren Bradley's death, the Randolphs quietly placed their home on the market and left Sausalito for the more tranquil and private life of Manhattan.

Two months later news raced through town that a dot-com CEO, Patricia Smith, and her husband Mario had purchased the Randolph home.

On the week they arrived and settled in, Oscar and Clarice Anderson came to welcome their new neighbors bringing a plate of cherry fudge brownies.

The successful young couple invited them in. When Patricia Smith took her first bite of the heavenly brownies introduced to Clarice by the Gossiping Gourmet, she exclaimed, "These are delicious! Do you mind giving me the recipe?"

Clarice hesitated and considered her response. For just a

brief moment, the image of Warren standing at her doorstep holding his brownies, anxious for her to share what she and Oscar knew about the Randolphs, flashed through her mind.

Finally, Clarice smiled and said, "I'm happy to, my dear. It's an old recipe that has been in my family for years."

THE END

NOVELS IN THE MURDER IN MARIN
SERIES

The Gossiping Gourmet

(Book 1)

The Wicked Wife

(Book 2)

The Phantom Photographer

(Book 3)

The Terrible Teacher

(Book 4)

The Horrible Husband

(Book 5)

Coming 2019

NEXT UP!

THE WICKED WIFE
(Book 2)

When billionaire William Adams—Belvedere's most eligible widower—marries international superstar model Willow Wisp, local society's leading women are dismayed. After all, she half his age and, in their view, not interested in anything other than his money!

Like everyone else, newspaper publisher Rob Timmons, his assistant, Holly Cross, and his childhood friend, Sheriff's Detective, Eddie Austin, are baffled when Willow suddenly disappears.

Is she dead or simply hiding in some far flung corner of the world with one of her many rumored lovers? Or was she the victim of a cuckolded husband, who learned too late that his trophy bride was in truth, a very wicked wife?

The truth lies somewhere between the posh hotels of Paris, the dazzling parties of San Francisco, and the lush green hills of Marin.

HOW TO REACH MARTIN

Martin Brown is an author and journalist whose articles on health and relationships have appeared in *Redbook, Playboy,* and *Complete Woman* magazines. He and his wife, novelist Josie Brown, live in the city of San Francisco, where their grown children and granddog also reside.

For more Murder in Marin mysteries visit:

murderinmarin.com

Or go here to quickly sign up for Martin's newsletter:

subscribepage.com/MartinBrownEletterSignUp

You can also find Martin at:

facebook.com/MartinBrownCA

twitter.com/MurderInMarin